CHRISTINA R. ADAMS

Gr8__Nate

First edition

Cover art by Alex Dickson

This book was professionally typeset on Reedsy.
Find out more at reedsy.com

Author's Advisory

Readers,

   Please be aware that this book contains graphic depictions of suicide attempts. Only read this if you feel fully mentally prepared to do so.

   This novel is intended to tell a story of growth and living through pain. It does **not** promote suicide.

   If you are considering ending your life, please reach out to a mental health professional.

   In the United States, you can contact the **Suicide and Crisis Lifeline** anytime by calling or texting **988,** or you can visit **www.988lifeline.org** to chat with a counselor online.

   For a more comprehensive international list of resources, I recommend visiting the International Association for Suicide Prevention website: **www.iasp.info**.

   You can make it through this.

   Love,

   Christina R. Adams

Dedication

To anyone who has ever felt like Nate and to anyone who has been someone's Rex.

Also, to the love of my life, Calab, for being my biggest supporter and the person who held my ladder while I climbed out of my pit. My dream would have never become a reality without you.

Dear Mother and Father...

Dear Mother and Father,

Or Marty...or Grace...

To whoever finds my fucking body,

As you can see, I have killed myself.

This has been a long time coming. I have never felt like I belonged here—not in this house, not in this family, not in this life.

Mom, you tried to show me love, but you cared more for the money and security that Father gave you than you cared for me, your son. You tried to be genuine, and maybe you cared at some point, but when you said, "I love you," it sounded empty. The conflicted look in your eyes told me what you actually meant: "I'm *supposed* to love you."

Father, I know I'm not what you had in mind for a son. I could never be, and I am not sorry for it. Not one bit. Thanks for feeding and clothing me and shit. I hope you burn in Hell. When this is made public, I hope the whole city learns what a horrible villain you truly are.

Marty and Grace, thank you for being the only people who seemed to care for me. I apologize if one of you finds me.

-Nate

P.S. Burn my body and don't keep my ashes in this house.

1

Graduation (Part 1)

Lightning strike. Buff. Toxic blast. Parry. Shocking bolt.

And the boss is dead.

Bing. A new message pops up in the party chat.

Q-Rex: "We got his ass!"

Gr8_nate: "Hell yeah, man!"

It's not like we haven't run this raid a thousand times before. I've memorized how to counter all of the Obsidian Lord's attacks.

I glance at the time in the corner of the computer screen: 3:56 p.m.

Gr8_nate: "Shit! I have to get off. I'm going to be late for my graduation if I stay on much longer. I'll be back on tonight unless Rylee wants to hang out."

Q-Rex: "Congrats, man! Ttyl."

I gather my rewards for completing the raid and sell the junk I don't need.

Esc. Logout.

The screen changes back to my desktop. The background is a selfie of Rylee and me at Spawnpoint Lounge. We were having coffee after I fucked her off the walking trail at Wayfield Park. We could have come back to my place to fool around since it is almost always parent-free. But the park was right by the school, and let's face it, sneaking around is more fun.

I check my phone notifications, and a feeling of dismay threatens to pull my heart to my stomach. She still hasn't responded to me.

Other than the hum of my computer fans, the house is soundless. The housekeeper, Grace, must have already gone home. My parents are going to meet me at the auditorium later. My father is going to the academy straight from work, and my mother will be coming from whatever appointment or shopping is filling her day.

Groaning, I get up from my desk chair, where I have had my ass planted for the last six hours. If I have to participate in this miserable ceremony, I should try to look like I haven't been dungeon-busting with Rex all day.

I stretch my back and roll my shoulders as I scuff my way to my walk-in closet. Despite my usual rotation of clothes only including two pairs of cargoes, five t-shirts, a pair of jeans, a hoodie, and whatever boxers happen to be sitting at the top of my drawer, my closet is *packed* with clothes. They are only taking up space. I haven't even taken the tags off most of them.

My mother *desperately* wants me to conform to my father's appearance-obsessed lifestyle, so she shops and shops until I decide I'll wear them. I sift through the unworn clothes and decide on a pair of dark gray slacks. Mom bought the pants for the ribbon-cutting ceremony for Father's new building. It turns out I wasn't invited to attend. They aren't my style, but I figure I should get some use out of them. This seems like an appropriate occasion. The tag's still on. Jesus Christ. $225.

I don't understand why my parents insist on these name brands. Regardless of my father's social status and being the most sought-after architect in Boston, our family doesn't have a lot of publicity. At least *I* don't. My parents will attend galas and parties, but not me. I don't need these fancy clothes. All I need are my school uniforms, my usual day-to-day wear, and something to stay warm in the winter. My mother still holds out hope that my father will invite me to be part of his perfect picture. Not that I would accept the invitation anyway.

I shuffle through the closet again and find a black button-down shirt with a faint, dark gray chevron print. Yet another piece of clothing bought by my mother for an event my father didn't let me attend. This shirt was supposed to be for my grandfather's funeral. He was an old bastard just like my father, and also a well-known Bostonian socialite. There were bound to be photographers present. My father didn't need me to tarnish the Whims family image in local magazines and newspapers.

I cross my room to the attached bathroom and give myself a once-over in the mirror. I wonder when I will finally start looking more like a man rather than the baby-faced boy peering back at me. I fiddle with my espresso brown, curly hair. It was once a tailored cut, faded on the sides, and piled up a bit on top. Exactly the way Mom likes it. Prim, but still youthful. It's a bit overgrown now. I don't mind, but I am a tad surprised Mom hasn't made me get it cut. After all, I am graduating from high school today, and *we must always look our best*. My sparse facial hair could use a shave, and I should brush my teeth, but other than that, I am ready to get this over with.

It's nearly 4:30 p.m. My bus is scheduled to arrive in about 15 minutes, so there is plenty of time to get out the door and to the bus stop. I take my time walking down the dark wooden stairs to the entryway and enable the alarm system before shutting the front door behind me. Code: 7913. The four corners of the keypad. My parents aren't very clever, but at least it is easy to remember and wouldn't be a burglar's *very* first guess.

This neighborhood is historic and nice to look at. One of the few perks of having a *"visionary"* as a father is that he can afford a decent place and has excellent taste.

One of the many downsides to having a *"visionary"* as a father is that I've had *"design"* and *"attention to detail"* shoved down my throat since I was a damn toddler. Apparently, this was to prepare me for taking over my father's firm when he retires. On my 16th birthday, I told him I didn't want to follow in his footsteps. He was not surprised in the least. He only said he was relieved that I decided on my own, so he didn't have to kick me out of the arrangement himself and be forced to withstand my mother's scorn.

Despite my distaste for architecture, I can't help but admire the beauty of the Victorian-era houses as I walk down the street to the bus stop. They are wooden and ornate. The current homeowners are much different than the original ones. Luxury cars are parked in each paved driveway instead of gravel spaces for horse-drawn buggies. Now surveillance cameras are at each front door, as opposed to people not being thieving ass hats. I'm sure there was crime during that time. You know, like Jack the fucking Ripper, but it seems like they at least had more faith in humanity than we do now. I'm just a kid; as my father likes to remind me, what do I even know about the world *or* the people in it?

Jesus Christ. What the fuck is wrong with me? I was just thinking about the houses, and, *choo-choo,* my train of thought arrives at Serial Killer Station.

I plop down on the bench at the bus stop and pull out my phone. 4:38 p.m. Great, I have seven minutes to spare. There are seven minutes to wait in silence.

I bounce my leg up and down. I try to focus on the text-based RPG I'm playing on my phone.

I have been able to distract myself with Rex and the houses. Now that I am alone and sitting still, it seems my intrusive thoughts have been taken over by my awful attention span.

I notice a stray piece of thread on the hem of my slacks. Why hasn't Rylee texted me back? I tug at the loose thread and read the description of the encounter for the third time.

She has been acting distant lately. Is that what she wants? Distance? She will get it soon. There is *plenty* of distance between Boston and the Quilliard School of Arts, where she will be starting school in the fall. She probably can't wait to get away from my miserable ass anyway. How she has stayed with me for so long is a complete enigma.

I shake my head at the thought. No, I shouldn't assume she is going to break up with me. She could have a perfectly good explanation for ignoring me. I start nibbling on my too-short fingernails.

This is why I like to keep busy. My hands, legs, and mind all want to keep moving. Stay busy. That's why I plan ahead and schedule my time like I do. There is no time in between. No buffer. Just. Keep. Moving.

I don't know what I am going to do next. I'm nervous about tonight and only feel dread about the coming days. Tomorrow, I wake up with no goal. There is no finish line to run toward. I'm careful about planning everything, but not this. Not my future.

5

Why did I do this? How did I let this slip by? I've wasted all this fucking time.

I can feel my upper lip begin to sweat despite the mild spring afternoon. I bounce my leg faster. Faster.

I can feel my heart beating in my ears.

I close my eyes and try to remember what the school counselor said to do when I feel like this.

I steady my breathing.

Right, grounding. Think of three things that ground me and give me purpose.

I have my friends. And not one of them offered to pick me up for graduation. Dickheads.

I have Rylee. As of right now, anyway.

The next storyline update is coming to *Realm of Battlecraft* in a few days. That is definite.

Even after Rylee moves, with *R.O.B.*, my summer will be well-filled. But after the summer, what—my interior monologue is halted by the squeal of a bus coming to a stop in front of me. The hiss of the air brakes sounds like a sigh of relief to these anxious ears.

Finally.

I find a seat and pull my phone out of my pocket once more. Just 10 minutes, and I'll be at the academy.

I scroll through my old texts from Rylee.

She hasn't sent me more than a three-word response in nearly a week. She hasn't responded to the text I sent yesterday afternoon. I have not seen her at all during the week-long break between final exams and graduation. What could she be doing? Why? Why hasn't she responded? Maybe I don't want to explore the possibilities.

Haunted by the thought, I can't help but imagine it. Her

soft, pale skin. Red, wavy hair that flows just past her shoulder blades. Freckles under her soft, blue eyes. Her eyes are what drew me to her to begin with. In those eyes, I could completely lose myself. She captivates everyone with a single look because of her effortless charm and ease. It is something I have been both envious of and enamored by since we were in kindergarten. All that beauty is wrapped around such a kind heart, but I can still see her in someone else's arms. Someone strong and more attractive. Someone with prospects.

Compared to her incredible talent and beauty, I seem so unremarkable. I am not worthy of her. I have no aspirations. Maybe she has been talking to someone who can be something more for her than I can. She is incredible. She shone like a literal fucking star in the last school play. She has been accepted to the most prestigious arts school in the country. If she hasn't already found someone, I'm sure she will when she moves to New York.

I have no artistic talent or leadership skills. No physical prowess or book smarts. How I got into such an elite academy is beyond comprehension. She deserves the world, and I can give her nothing.

I'm worthless. My father has reminded me of that fact at least once a month since I started Buchanan Academy, even more often in the months leading up to graduation.

My heart pounds even faster.

Graduation. She has to be there. I will have to see her to get the answers I need. Even if I don't deserve her, she is my best friend and owes me an explanation for ignoring me.

Fuck.

She is going to be there. She is *definitely* going to be there. Fuck. I can't face it. She has been everything to me for so long.

7

Maybe it would be better not to know. I could jump off the bus at the next stop. Run home. Curl up in bed. Die.

The bus squeals to a halt near the front gates of the academy. This time, the release of air from the brakes feels more like a terrified gasp than a sigh of relief. I can see her through the window. She has been waiting for me. I can't avoid her now.

I walk to the exit and am overwhelmed by a sense of dread. She is going to leave me; I know it. My legs feel heavy. Sluggish. My heart is yelling at me to run and prevent the inevitable pain. But, with shaky legs, I move forward despite it.

As I descend the steps, she comes a couple of steps closer with an adorable smile slanted across her face. My heart feels like it is pumping so hard it could burst. I wipe my finger over my upper lip. Am I visibly sweating?

"Hey, cutie!" she shouts as she bounds over to me and softly kisses my cheek. I want to pull back and ask why the hell she hasn't been talking to me, but instead, I pull her into my arms and squeeze her.

Maybe I have been overthinking again.

I step away, holding her hands in mine, and look her up and down. "You look beautiful, babe."

I take in the image of her. Her usually wavy hair is curled into loose spirals; her yellow dress is vibrant under her sky blue graduation gown; and her light make-up makes her look like sweet, youthful innocence given form. Not that she is innocent. I've heard those light pink lips cussing like a sailor during her gaming streams. I've seen those same lips painted brick red and wrapped around my dick.

I warned her that night that dark lipstick always makes guys think about blow jobs. She saw that as an invitation to undo my pants. Of course, that was my intention all along.

8

I look away and think of a freezing day, roadkill, split pea soup—anything to help avoid the embarrassment of a public erection. Despite the hefty price tag, these pants are made of awfully thin fabric.

Until now, I've managed to get through high school without making a complete fool of myself. I don't need it to happen during graduation at all times.

"Hey, guys!" I turn and see Ashley walking over from the student parking lot.

Well, that takes care of the erection.

Ashley may be Rylee's best friend, but she disgusts me. She acts as if I am the enemy, and Rylee is some sort of prize to acquire. Ashley also got accepted to a school in New York, so I guess she will finally have Rylee all to herself.

Congratulations, you possessive bitch; you won.

"Hey, Ashe." She gives me a little smile and grabs Rylee's hand, pulling her toward the academy. "We need to find our spots in line for the procession. We are running late!" Rylee is yanked away, but she looks over her shoulder, offers me an apologetic smile, and shouts, "Let's meet back here after graduation."

Shit. Is that when she plans to break my heart? She is going to wait until after the ceremony so that I can stew on it through the whole infernal thing.

I hear laughter as my other friends, Liam, Hayden, and Dominic, arrive. I wave goodbye to Rylee and say, "See you then."

The guys and I walk toward the orchestra room, where students with a last name starting with letters L through Z are to line up.

"So, I guess you guys weren't able to pick me up?" I glance

9

towards Dominic, who only lives two blocks from me.

"No, it's not that; we are all going out to dinner with our families afterward. It didn't make sense to pick you up since we aren't going back home after the ceremony."

"Well, my parents are bringing me home anyway, so it wouldn't have mattered."

They exchange glances but say nothing. A moment passes before Liam finally changes the subject. "I am so pumped for the R.O.B. update," he says. "I can't believe they are adding a new playable race after all this time." The rest of us mumble our agreement.

He sensed his attempt to change the subject had failed, so he began rambling about his plans for after graduation. I tune him out. Liam hates silence. I get it. It is odd, though, that Hayden and Dominic are also quiet. They are two of the rowdiest people I know. Maybe they are just nervous about graduating. Or maybe they already know my world is about to end.

I am certainly anxious. I have to walk across the stage not only in front of students who won't recognize me as anyone other than 'Rylee's boyfriend' but also their parents, some of the most powerful people in this city. What if I fall? God. I'll have to move, that's for sure, maybe across the country.

As we approach the auditorium, Hayden and Liam split off toward the choir practice room, where Ashe and Rylee most likely had already found their places in the A through K line, leaving Dominic and me to walk to the orchestra room in silence. The silence is only fractured by my never-broken-in shoes squeaking on the waxed marble floor, making the walk even more uncomfortable.

An announcement sounds over the school's speaker system: "Graduates! To your places! The procession begins in *one* minute!"

We take off, running to the opposite end of the marble hall. We make it to the orchestra room with only seconds to spare. I nod goodbye to Dominic as he heads toward the middle of the line to find his place among the 'Rs'. To find my place among the "Ws," I walk and walk and walk a little bit faster to nearly the end of the line.

I only have a couple of moments to take in the room. I haven't been in this room since the end of my first school year. I was called into the director's office and politely asked to register for a different course to satisfy my artistry credit for the next school year. I had no objections. I found the abstract art instructor much more accepting of my lack of artistic talent.

Today, the room isn't silent and awkward like that day with the director. The room is buzzing with the excited murmurs of 150 students. It ties my stomach in a knot. I wish I had time to use the bathroom.

The orchestra begins to play, and we walk. Thankfully, the music mostly drowns out the sound of my squeaking shoes. By the time we reach the auditorium, my shoes are completely hushed by the orchestra playing "Pomp and Circumstance" and the applauding crowd.

As I find my seat, I glance around the room in search of familiar faces. I notice the faces of people I have known since before I started school, yet I feel no connection to them. They are mostly the children of my father's associates. During elementary school, I was forced to go on *play dates*, as my mother called them. Once a week, the same group of kids would meet at one of our houses to play. It was just an excuse for our mothers to get wine-drunk together on Tuesday evenings while someone's nanny kept an eye on all of us. It is how I met Rylee for the first time. We hit it off, and our parents took it from there.

I take a seat, but twist in my chair to scan the crowd for my parents. I quickly turn back around when I see that Rylee's father is sitting just two rows behind me. I can feel his stare piercing into the nape of my neck. I'm sure he notices my unkempt hair and shirt, slightly wrinkled from years of being stuffed in my closet.

I feel his eyes staring daggers into my back, and as if the daggers are laced with them, I can hear his thoughts. *Nate is worthless. He doesn't deserve my daughter. Despite having no other children, his father won't let this boy inherit his company. How can he support her and keep her happy? He is a pathetic waste of oxygen.* The thoughts make me dizzy and nauseated. Maybe that is just the ever-constricting knot of anxiety in my stomach.

"Welcome, graduates and families!" The class president's voice spares me from imagining what else Rylee's father might be pondering. "We are so excited to have all of you here today as we celebrate the great accomplishments of these brilliant young men and women."

I settle into my seat and focus on the speaker's words, only to avoid getting caught up in the dark chasm of my mind.

"It is a joyous day for many of you, but also a day full of sorrow for some. We journey out into this world searching for our dreams, but we leave good friends behind to find these greener pastures. This makes today a truly bittersweet event."

I roll my eyes. Oh, so it's going to be like that? Phony, heartfelt speeches about how we have become better people in our years at Buchanan and made friends along the way, and blah blah blah. It's infuriating.

Here's one positive thing about tomorrow: I won't have to

12

deal with this bullshit anymore.

I risk glancing over my shoulder. Rylee's dad, Mr. Dunwall, is staring me dead in the eye, expressionless, like he despises me wholly. The man is terrifying. I feel goosebumps rise on my arms, and my hair stands up on the back of my neck. I casually face the speaker again and vow to stare straight ahead until the ceremony is over.

2

Graduation (Part 2)

"Ladies and Gentlemen, I present to you this year's Buchanan Academy graduating class." The audience applauds as the dean wraps up her closing speech.

About damn time. It has been an eternal hour of half-hearted, pandering speeches.

It's a marvel how the student body president, a state senator's son, no doubt bound for politics himself, could accent his speech perfectly with a well-placed pause as if considering his own rhetorical questions. Or even more awe-inspiring, the valedictorian's perfectly rehearsed sniffle and soft-spoken apology crap. As if that sniveling mayor's daughter would actually shed tears for this miserable place. There isn't a doubt in my mind that their parents hired professional speech writers to compose this bullshit and then coach them on how to deliver each word, pause, smile, and sniffle *perfectly*.

That insufferable hour was followed by the rattling off of names, most of which I didn't recognize. Well, I didn't recognize their first names. You would have to live far beneath the city not to recognize their last names. The same last names belong to some of Boston's richest men and women.

We throw our caps in the air. The cheers of the graduates echo through the auditorium. For a fleeting second, I feel like I might join them in their excitement, but then I take in what surrounds me. I see smiling faces; some people are hugging. Shit. Some people are even *crying*. For what? Leaving behind friends who they won't even think about a year from now? Will they be missing the seven hours a day of incessant lectures and diligent note-taking? No. Their guises are unconvincing, and I have no reason to celebrate with them.

I stare down at my cap for a moment and debate whether or not to leave it there.

I snatch my cap off the ground and press my way through a group of squealing girls who seem completely unaware they are blocking the entire aisle. I haven't noticed my parents yet, but that is a good thing. I have somewhere else to be before I meet up with them.

I need to talk to Rylee.

But first, I have to find the bathroom.

The sea of people in the auditorium looks nearly impassable, so I opt to use the bathroom behind the stage instead of the one in the hall by the entrance. I quicken my pace and dash into the first open stall I see.

Thankfully, I am in here alone. I don't have to feel self-conscious about anyone hearing me take a shit.

But then, I hear the door squeak open, followed by the sound of two faint voices. There goes my hopes of getting through my anxiety shits in peace.

As they come further into the restroom, the voices become clearer. "I feel bad for the guy, though."

Wait. I know that voice. I peek through the gap in the stall

15

door. I can see the wheels of Hayden's wheelchair by the sinks.

"I know, and I guess I do too. A little bit. I don't blame her, though; the guy is a loser." And that is unmistakably Liam's voice.

I hear Hayden sigh and say, "He is a nice guy, and I feel bad for him. When is she going to do it?"

The voices sound like they are getting farther away.

"She is probably doing it right now," Liam replies.

I hear silence and look through the crack in the door again. They are gone.

The world feels as if it is spinning faster and faster. My blood is frozen. My whole body is *frozen*. I knew it. I fucking knew it. What they said... They must have been talking about Rylee and me. She is going to abandon me. She is going to leave me behind and— something hot begins to churn inside me. I break out in a cold sweat and barely spin around in time to barf into the toilet.

I sit back down on the toilet and rest my head on my hands, trying to steady myself. My world is spiraling out of control. It is one thing to have a hunch about something happening, but to have it confirmed, especially by someone else, is another thing entirely. By the sound of it, I was going to be the last person to find out.

I struggle to take in air as I fail to steady my breathing. Maybe I am just reading into it. They could be talking about anyone. How vain I am, just assuming they are talking about me.

No, they were definitely talking about me.

I want to scream. I want to punch out all the bathroom mirrors and sob on the floor. Roll around in the shards of glass. Something. Something to make this go away.

The only way I can move past it is first to let the horrible thing happen. I'll give myself five more minutes—just five more minutes to collect myself.

* * *

I'm terrified and feel like I could hurl again at any moment, but I keep a steady pace as I walk to the spot where Rylee wants to meet. I've felt this coming for a while now. I just need to let it happen, so I can start pulling myself back together. I've got this. I can handle this.

I can't handle it. I can't. My breath becomes shallow, and my ears become heated. I can see her in the distance. She is already waiting for me. She is chatting with Ashe, who has her hand on her shoulder. Her expression is serious as she meets my eyes over Rylee's graduation cap. She gives my girlfriend a quick hug before taking off toward the student parking lot.

Rylee turns to me, and I am horrified. That is sympathy within her beautiful eyes. I stop in my tracks.

She crosses the few feet between us and gives me a weak hug. I hear a ringing in my head. The air feels thin. I should never have let go of her when she hugged me before graduation. We could have stood there forever. Lived and died there.

"You're breaking up with me." I manage to get out.

She pulls away from our embrace, and I notice a gleam in her eye. "You're smart, Nate. Despite what you say, you are intelligent. I will be moving soon. I'll be hours away, and after I graduate from college, who knows where I will go? California? That's even farther." Her words were composed and serious.

"But I love you." The ringing in my ears turns into TV static. This isn't happening.

I can see tears welling in her eyes. She pushes a strand of hair

17

out of her face and wraps her arms around herself.

"I know you do. I love you too. Just trust me when I say it needs to be this way."

She wants me to accept it just like that? Hell no.

"Why? I could come with you and-"

"And what, Nate? What would you do in New York? Get a minimum-wage job to support yourself. Do you know how expensive it is to live there? My dad is paying for my apartment, but he won't pay for me to *shack up* with my boyfriend. His words, not mine."

I step closer to her and lower my voice. "Well, why does he have to know? We won't tell him, and you can dress me in some disguise if he comes for a visit." I give her a teasing smile.

Please remember why you like me. I'm cute and sweet. I'm funny. You've said these things to me a thousand times. *Remember.*

She gives me a frank, unamused look.

"Rylee, I am joking. We can work and support ourselves. We can get by without his help."

She goes still for a moment, as if considering what she is about to say carefully. "Please, Nate. It has to be like this. You have nothing lined up for you in New York. I have school to focus on. When I am not in school, I will have dance lessons, vocal coaching, and a part-time job. I will let my dad pay for my apartment, but I sure as hell won't ask the man for an allowance."

"Oh, so is this about your independence? Relying on one another wouldn't make you any less independent. I mean, technically, we would be co-dependent, but you would still be free of trying to constantly live up to his ridiculous standards if I'm paying half the bills."

She straightens, and in a tone I have never heard from her, she says, "I have to do this alone."

My own tone becomes desperate, pleading, "Rylee, I don't know what I did or what..."

She interrupts, "I don't want to hurt you, Nate, but I will say anything I have to for you to accept this and just let me go." She is unmovable.

The roaring inside my head goes silent. I chuckle, back up a step, and open my arms. "Take the shot, Rylee. Just fucking say it."

She lets out a huff and furrows her brow slightly. I know that look. She is pissed. Oh man, is she pissed. And I know it is out of that anger that she spews what her father rants about at least once a week at their family dinners, occasionally while I am present.

"You have no goals. You are doing nothing after we leave here tonight. Nothing tomorrow. I am moving. I want a life of adventures and success, but I can't have those things with you dragging behind me. You're content to stay in Boston for the rest of your life. Content to live your life only caring about new game releases and wasting your time with me. This city and game nights together might be enough for you, but it isn't enough for me." And maybe to kill any fight I had left, she finishes with, "*You* aren't enough for me."

There it is—the killing blow.

My heart shatters. I've died. I am in Hell.

"Goodbye, Rylee." I turn in the direction of the school's front entrance and start walking; my legs feel like they shouldn't be able to hold me.

She sniffs. "Goodbye, Nate."

That sniff. The wavering in her voice. She is crying, but I

19

don't look back. Despite my chest feeling so heavy it could drag me to the ground, I straighten my posture to look a bit less defeated in case she is watching. She just utterly destroyed me, but I will be damned if she sees how much damage she has done.

As soon as I am out of her sight, I let go of my bogus composure. I don't know how I am still standing.

After what feels like an eternity, I reach the spot where I am to meet my parents. I sit down on the sidewalk and let what just happened sink in.

She is incredible, and I can never measure up. I failed. I've failed at everything. I will never amount to a goddamn thing. The person who means the most to me just took all of my insecurities, loaded them into a gun, and shot them at me over and over again. No goals. Wasting my time. Dragging behind. Not enough. Not enough. Not enough.

She came at me like a tornado and tore down the massive wall I carefully constructed between me and everyone else. Every feeling I have been avoiding—the panic and insecurities I push down daily—they're spilling out, and I am *drowning* in them. I cross my arms on my knees, rest my head on my arms, and weep.

Celebrating, laughing people walk around me while I am stooped and sobbing on the sidewalk. Minutes pass, and the tears finally stop as I notice it has become mostly silent. I look up from where I am sitting to see that the parking lot is almost empty. My father's car is nowhere to be seen.

I run back inside to see only janitors cleaning the auditorium and a few families with chatty, doting mothers still taking pictures.

The sadness and hopelessness that once consumed me are

now replaced with an empty space. I feel nothing. Not angry. Not surprised. Nothing. My parents somehow forgot their only child's graduation. I truly have been abandoned.

I drag myself back to the curb, where I see a black sedan and a man in a suit standing by the passenger side door.

He offers a friendly smile and says, "Mr. Whims."

"Did my father hire you to kill me? You would be doing me a service at this point, so I should be the one paying you." He looks a tad surprised but seems mostly untroubled by my bizarre question.

"Uh... no. I'm from Luxury Rides Driving Service. I apologize for my late arrival. I was only just notified of your need for a ride."

"How did you know that I am *Mr. Whims*?" I say my name in a sarcastically pretentious tone. "And I suppose my parents are not with you."

He bites his lip but grins. "I received a rough description of your appearance. It also helps that you are the only person out here. Your parents are not with me. I only know where to pick you up and where to drop you off. So, if you have no other questions..." He trails off, but opens the rear passenger side door.

I slide into the backseat. "Damn, so you really aren't here to kill me?" He shook his head and shut the door a little harder than necessary.

I check my phone, hoping to see a text from Rylee begging for my forgiveness and to take her back. I have a single message.

Mom: "Sorry, your car was late, honey! Congratulations, my little graduate!"

I'm not ready to respond to her, so I put my phone in my pocket and lean my head against the cool window.

The driver and I pass the ride in silence, which gives me time to sort through my conversation with Rylee. She didn't seem like she was lying to me, but she is such a damn good actress that I probably wouldn't have been able to pick up on signs that she *was* lying. But those tears, the earnestness in her voice and eyes when she asked me to simply accept the fact that our relationship *had* to end. There was something else. She almost seemed mournful.

I suppose mourning would be appropriate. We have been dating for almost four and a half years, and she has been my best friend since we were children. Rylee has always been with me.

The feeling of hopelessness begins to snake its way through my veins again, and I feel icy as I am overcome by dread.

This is worse than the distress I feel trying to figure out my life plan. This is the terror of being trapped in a room with no air. This is the panic of something you know you need to survive being stripped away. There is no way of knowing how long you can survive without it, but you know there is an inevitable, painful end coming.

The car rolls to a stop in front of the house. All the lights I had left on before leaving are casting a yellow glow from the windows. I wave goodbye to the driver as he pulls away and make my way to the front door. As I enter the quiet house, I shout, "Mom? Dad?" Silence.

I make my way to the kitchen. I'm absolutely starved since I haven't eaten anything besides a cup of ramen for lunch. Again, I shout for Mom or Dad—still nothing.

There is a bottle of something on the counter. A neatly folded piece of paper sits next to it with my first name written in bold, capital letters on the outer fold. My father's handwriting. I unfold it, and inside:

Nate,

Your mother and I found an earlier flight for our trip to Europe. We had to take it as your mother insists on making it in time for the final days of the tulip festival in the Netherlands. I am deeply sorry we missed your graduation. I have transferred $5,000 into your checking account for groceries or eating out. That should get you by for the next few months without us, but if you need more, text me. Congratulations on graduating, son.

–Dad

P.S. Your mom left you something in the fridge.

I guess that explains why nobody cheered when my name was called at graduation.

Well, at least there is food, and I read the label on the bottle, sparkling cider. Fuck. If they were going to do this shit to me, they could have at least given me some booze. They would rather attend a *tulip* festival than their only offspring's graduation. I wish I could say I'm surprised.

Sitting under the bottle is a Fuel gift card for $250. At least I don't have to spend any of my food money on new games. This should cover all the game releases I want this Summer.

I scoff. Games really are the only thing I live for now.

I open the fridge door, hoping to find some pad thai and spring rolls from that place I love down the road, but instead, I find a cake. A cake with little plastic balloons and graduation caps. And written in blue frosting: "Happy 18th Birthday, Nate."

I'm glad they remembered my birthday, but I turn 19 today.

A cake. A bottle of cider. $5,000. A ridiculously large, empty house. Abandoned.

I walk to my room and pull up ZoomEats on my computer.

I should at least have a decent dinner on my birthday. I order some Thai food and then pull up another tab.

Before I type anything into the search bar, my stomach pulls me back to the kitchen. I bring the cake, the bottle of cider, and an ornate silver fork back to my room.

That's right, Mom, I am using the good silverware to eat cake straight out of the container. You can't stop me from all the way across the Atlantic Ocean.

I lounge back in my desk chair and open the disappointing bubbly with a hardly satisfying *pop*.

"A toast to you on your special day, Nate." I sip directly from the bottle and dig into the cake with the fork. I sit up straight in my computer chair and begin typing in the search bar:

How to tie a noose.

3

Hangman's Knot

A noose is tied using a hangman's knot. So why the hell did we settle on calling it a noose? Hangman's snarl, lyncher's lariat, and gallow snare would all be better names. They sound like death metal bands. Noose. Pathetic. It sounds like when my two-year-old cousin tried to say goose.

I chuckle to myself, thinking about how excited he was about seeing the geese at the park, yet he ran straight back to me, screaming as soon as one honked at him. He is a sweet kid. His parents, my aunt and uncle on my mother's side, are not like mine. They are energetic, not worn down by the elevated expectations of the jet set. They weren't born into money like my father. They live humbly and are down-to-earth. I wish I had a family like that. I once pictured making my own with Rylee.

Instead, I get my father, a man who is concerned about his image to an absurd degree. He painted his life perfectly. With an adoring trophy wife, expensive European cars, and a lavish home, he had the life he had always dreamed of having. But my mother gave birth to me. I am the one thing wrong in my father's life. The smear on the perfect picture he imagined. He wanted a girl. A doll he could dress up and show off at parties. Someone he could set up with the finest lawyers' or bankers' sons, hoping to gain a business connection or possibly a new fortune from the match. It is the 21st century. Offspring shouldn't be seen as a source of income through marital bonds, but here we are.

The ring of the doorbell interrupts my wandering thoughts. I take my time walking to the front door to give the ZoomEats driver a chance to get back to their car. I pause at the door and peer through the peephole. I can see the silhouette of a man heading to his car. He is far enough away that I wouldn't be rude for not saying anything, so I open the door and snatch my meal off the front step.

When I turn toward the stairs, the liquor cart in the parlor catches the corner of my eye. As if I still don't believe the house is empty, I scan the room to be sure I am not being watched. Some vodka would greatly improve my *celebratory* cider. I cross the parlor and stoop in front of the walnut liquor cabinet. I reach for the brass handle, tug at it, and... it's locked. What the fuck?

I can't believe they chose this moment to be responsible parents. I've been drinking wine with dinner since I was 12 years old, and I was allowed one watered-down cocktail at Christmas since I was 16, but now, as an adult man, I cannot have a drink with dinner. I stand with a huff, grab my food, and head back up the stairs.

I notice the cake I placed beside my keyboard. I was so absorbed by my morbid research that I only ate a few bites. I pop the lid back on it, place my bag from Siam Noodles down, and begin laying the food out neatly on my desk: combination

Pad Thai, shrimp spring rolls, and two containers of peanut sauce. I take a hefty swig of the Thai tea that came with my meal and settle back into my chair. I click play on the video I left open on my computer.

Make a large U shape with your rope. Create a second U shape facing down. So, like a sideways S. *Your rope should now resemble a sideways S.* No shit. Everyone must feel like killing themselves after watching this video.

I need to eat my food before the noodles get cold.

I open another browser tab, pull up MakiRoll, and click on *Rice Balls Basket* under my *continue watching* list. I know it's considered a girls' anime, but I have seen it several times. It's my comfort show. It's mellow, and I don't care if I miss the subtitles while taking a bite of food. I know the story by heart.

By the end of the second episode, the White Day episode, I hit the bottom of my takeout container. I reach for the cake again and click *Next Episode*. This episode is about the first day of a new school term.

Since I am no longer in high school, is it weird for me to continue watching shows where the characters are?

I continue nibbling on the cake and clicking *Next Episode* until I can no longer keep my eyes open. I've eaten to the point of total exhaustion. I pop the lid back on the cake and turn off both monitors.

I undress down to my boxers, sprawl out on my king-size bed, and savor the slight burn as I stretch my limbs as far as they can. Sitting at a desk for hours isn't hard work, but it certainly makes me sore.

I take a deep breath and try to clear my mind. This is the most difficult time for me to relax. While trying to fall asleep, I have no distractions. With no distractions, I get trapped in my swirling thoughts. I get caught up in my errors. The things I should have said. The things I should have done.

I think back on that episode of *Rice Balls Basket*—the first day of a new school term. My first days of school are over. Life has always been a predictable cycle for me: school, summer break with Rylee and the guys, back to school, and back to summer break again. But now, my future is like an endless void. It is sucking me in, and I have no way to avoid the emptiness waiting inside.

My mother is not here to pester me with affection each evening after she has had three glasses of wine, feeling guilty for ignoring the way my father torments me. I have no girlfriend to hold me against her when I question myself and need reassurance. No light. No new assignment. No goal. No comfort.

I turn on my left side and sink into myself. I am trying to find my way out of a dark tunnel with no light shining at the end. Even if I find my way out, I'm still left in the dark.

A pressure begins to build in my chest. It slowly grows until it is intolerable. I survey my dark room, searching for something to ground myself before panic fully sets in.

My eyes are drawn to the only light in the room, the lights on my computer tower. Games and shows are my life now. That computer is my only source of companionship and entertainment. Am I supposed to live my life with only distractions for company until I inevitably conform to my father's perfect image of me?

Or am I to take control of my own future?

The image of the tab I left open flashes in my mind. There is a definite way to take control of my future. My dark tunnel ends here, with a cement wall crafted by my own hand.

I jump out of bed, but I don't head for my computer. I throw on the lounge pants I removed just moments ago. Barefoot, I sprint down the stairs to the back door. I don't stop running until I am through the French doors and nearly collide with the wooden shed.

Panting, I yank on the handle of the barn-style door, but it doesn't budge.

"Dammit, Marty!" I grumble as I slam my fist on the door.

I circle to the side of the shed and peer in through the lone window. A long coil of rope hangs neatly on the wall on the other side of the shed.

The window doesn't open. If I were to break it, I wouldn't even be able to fit my shoulders through it, so that's pointless. My options are to try to kick open the door or wait to ask Marty to open it with his copy of the key.

I don't see that conversation going very well.

"Hey, Marty, can you open the shed for me?"

"Sure. What do you need from the shed?"

"I need the rope."

"Why?"

"Oh, nothing major. I just want to hang myself."

"No problem, Nate. I'll even tie and hang the noose for you!"

Kicking down the door, it is.

I step back about three feet from the door and bring my right leg up to my chest. With all the strength I can muster, I slam my foot into the door next to the lock.

"Shit!"

My fucking ankle! I bounce a couple of times on my left leg and sputter, "God, dammit. I can't fucking—ugh!" then fall to the ground and examine my ankle. It doesn't look like I broke any bones, but I didn't bust open the door either.

I linger in the grass and let the night breeze clear my mind. I look back at the shed door and slam my palm against my forehead. I am such an idiot. I should have at least put on a pair of shoes. I turn toward the lights shining through the open kitchen door. There must be a viable substitute for the rope inside the house.

I return to my room and slump into my computer chair. In the dark, I sit back and consider my options.

I don't need an actual rope to hang myself, but what could I use instead? My scarf? That'll be too stretchy. A sheet might work, but I'm worried that it won't tighten very well, and I'll be stuck hanging in a noose that won't actually suffocate me. My only belt just broke, so that option is out.

I wonder if my mother doesn't buy me belts because it is her way of acknowledging that her perfect family will never be complete. Maybe she realizes that I will never actually fit, just like my pants, because I have no damn belt. Focus, Nate!

I turn to my computer to check a forum for suggestions, but as soon as I touch my mouse, it hits me. I kept my old wired mouse when I upgraded to wireless. I thought I'd keep it on hand in case I needed a backup. Or maybe I am just a hoarder.

Whatever, my hoarding is just another problem I won't have to worry about in a few minutes.

I open the lid to a plastic box, which, after a bit of searching, I found in the back of my closet. Sitting right on top of the pile of cords is my old mouse. I wrap the cord around my neck to get a feel for it. It is so thin. I doubt it would hold my weight, and if it did, it feels like it would damn near slice through my neck. If it were thicker, like a real rope, it would be more comfortable. I want to be dead, but I'd still like to die comfortably.

I sift through the box of chords again to find something

thicker. A coaxial cable, an HDMI cable, or an extension cord. Something to—wait, this could work.

I retrieve my old, wired keyboard from the box.

I sit back at my desk and tie the cords together right below the mouse and the keyboard, then twist the wires around each other. It's not a rope, but it should get the job done.

Again, I wrap it around my neck. It still doesn't feel great, but something about it feels right. I will live and die by the mouse and keyboard. I'll go eternally AFK.

I turn on my monitors and pull up the instructions for tying the knot. I form the S shape and pinch the curves together. I pass the end with the USBs behind the middle part of the squished S shape, and wrap it upwards again and again, five more times. I pass the USBs through what is left of the top loop and pull it tight.

It is such a simple process. Beautiful in a way that, I'd assume, only someone like me could appreciate. Maybe everyone who crafts this knot with the same intentions sees it as I do as I hold it up in my dim bedroom. In the light of my monitors, it looks like Heaven sent salvation.

For the first time in years, I feel hopeful. I'm pretty damn close to feeling excited. At the end of this rope hangs all that is expected of me: the harsh remarks of my father, the guilt of my mother, my dead-end future, and the love I still feel that isn't returned. Soon, I will be hanging from the end of this rope, and all of that will be gone.

I'm not sure when I first thought of killing myself, but it has been buzzing in the back of my mind for years. It might have been the first time my father called me "good for nothing". Or that time in third period when Scotty Fulton said I wasn't good enough for Rylee.

31

"Rylee is such a fine piece of ass. You know, when she finally realizes she is too good for you, all these guys..." He lazily gestured around the classroom with his pencil, "...will be lining up to fuck her. But I'll be first." Then, he laughed like he was merely joking around with a friend.

At first, I was pissed. I wanted to punch that fucker in the face, but combined with my own self-loathing, that anger turned into a three-day stay in a pit of depression. That was when I considered stabbing myself repeatedly with a Santoku knife.

While lost in thought, I walk to the center of my room. I manage to throw the long end of the cord over one of the beams suspended under the vaulted ceiling. I pass the loop through a circle I tied on the end of the cord. I grab the cable just above the knot and tug down on it several times. It feels secure.

I notice an ache in my right ankle as I step onto the chest at the foot of my bed. I turn to face my salvation. It's right at eye level. My neck can't break at this height, but I'll pass out from lack of oxygen soon enough. I slip the noose over my head and tighten it around my neck.

I pause a moment to glance around the room one last time. I don't feel any sadness about leaving this place behind. I'm setting all of us free by letting it all go—letting my life go.

I close my eyes and picture the first time I kissed Rylee—an awkward dare gone right, at least for a while. I think back to when I took her virginity. It was a beautiful day. I was so nervous, but from then on, I was never nervous or self-conscious around her. Not until tonight, that is.

For a moment, I am back at the bus stop at the academy. I can see her tearing up and hear her voice as clearly as I hear the whir of my computer fans: "You're not good enough."

I take a long step off the chest.

My stomach churns at the falling sensation, but I fall farther than expected and hit the floor.

"Fucking hell!" On the ground in front of me lies the tail end of the noose, and the knot I made to secure it to the beam is completely untied.

I tie a triple knot to secure the circle this time, toss it over the beam, pass the deadly end through it, and tug it down.

This time, it will have to work.

Once again, I step onto the chest and face the noose. This time, my mind is clear. All I feel is desperation and determination. I place the loop over my head, tug it tight, and take another long step of the chest.

I take a short fall. And with a jolt, I stop.

A tight, searing pain encircles my neck as the loop constricts steadily.

I have never realized how heavy my body is. And all that weight pulling on my neck—well, I feel like that cider bottle, and my head is the cork. *Pop.*

A dizzy, anxious feeling takes over. I'm lightheaded. I can't inhale at all.

An immense pressure builds in my head; there is too much blood. The blood has to get out somehow. Maybe out of my eyes or ears. Maybe the pressure will blast my skull open.

A coldness is creeping up my limbs, but from the tightening knot up, I am scorching.

"I can't breathe," I attempt to say, but no sound comes from my lips. I don't know why I feel the urge to say anything at all. Nobody is here. Nobody is coming. I'm alone. I'm going to die alone.

The air thins. I feel hot and cold. I grasp my throat and claw at the entwined wires. I kick as hard as I can, as if it can save me. My thrashing only makes the cords clench.

My vision blurs, and a dark haze encroaches around me. All I can hear is my lazy pulse and a whooshing sound in my skull.

Soon, it will be over. I'll be painless. I'll be free.

In the haze, I see my mom as I saw her when I was a little boy. I see my aunt, uncle, and little cousin. I see my childhood dog. I see Dominic and Hayden. I see a blurry figure with Rex's gaming tag floating above its head. I see Rylee's smile and shining eyes. One by one, the ghosts of my life fade away as my vision becomes darker

I cease clutching at my throat. My pounding headache is subsiding, and my anxiety shifts into a peaceful feeling I have never experienced before. I feel pure relief and acceptance.

I'm dying.

This is what I want.

I can no longer see a trace of my room. The whooshing turns to silence, and then—a crash.

* * *

I open my eyes and glance around, hardly moving my head. Small shards of wood surround my collapsed body. The headache has returned, but the weight on my neck is gone. The burning pain, however, remains.

Pain. Fuck. I'm alive.

I reach up, tug the cords loose and over my head, and slowly push myself into a sitting position. To my right, the beam has crashed and splintered to the floor.

"Fuck." My voice is just a guttural whisper.

I rub my head and neck, then slowly rise. I have never had a migraine like this. I stumble to the bathroom and shove my hand into the cabinet. I shake two painkillers into my palm.

I limp over to my desk, grab the cider, and swallow the pills. The carbonation sears as it goes down my throat.

My phone lights up. A text from Mom: "I hope graduation went well, sweetie!" I toss my phone onto my bed.

I walk straight through the splinters of wood to the bathroom again. I don't recognize who I see in the mirror. My eyes are bloodshot, and a red ring encircles my neck. I look down—oh, I pissed myself.

Slowly, I peel off my soiled clothes and turn on the shower. I stare myself down in the mirror. Disgusting. Pathetic. Worthless. I can't even kill myself. I glare at and scrutinize myself until the room fills with steam.

I step into the shower and breathe in the humidity. My lungs are quivering as they struggle to draw in the air. It is an agonizing process, but I manage to wash my hair and body. I lean against the tile and let the hot water flow over my aching muscles. I stare at the bottom of the shower, watching reddish-pink water pool around the drain for a while before finally convincing myself to move again.

I make my way back to my bed, not bothering to find under-wear or pajamas. I pick up my phone and finally respond to my mother's text. "Great night. Thanks for the cake." And collapse into my bed. I peer over the side and see the beam lying on the floor. It is a blinding reminder of my failure. Fuck it. That mess is tomorrow's problem.

I fall asleep to the sound of my wheezing breath and my heartbeat pounding in my ears.

4

A New Routine

The morning sun is dim, but it burns my eyes like it is shining right outside my bedroom window. My head is filled with a metallic ringing as I head toward the medicine cabinet to retrieve both ibuprofen and acetaminophen. I pop off the lids, toss a couple of each into my mouth, and place the still-open bottles on the counter. I return to my bed and drop onto my disheveled bedsheets.

I reach for my phone to check the time. Saturday, May 10th, 5:38 a.m. One new message. I turn off the screen, close my eyes, and crash.

* * *

I blink my eyes open. My cell is balanced on my open palm. I open a single eye, tap the screen twice, and check the time. 11:42 a.m. It's late. Not that there is anything I have to do or any place I need to be. I turn to lie on my back and stare straight at the ceiling where the wooden beam once hung. I debate staying in bed for the rest of the day, but instead, I sit up, the motion making my head spin. I rub my temples and then the back of my neck. The migraine I had hours ago has dulled into a gnarly headache. An improvement, but barely. I glance over the foot of my bed to take in the mess that still lies on the floor. Splintered wood and a crudely crafted noose are the remaining evidence of my pitiful attempt to end my life.

"Right." The word comes out muted and half-formed.

I clear my throat and move slowly to the edge of the bed, each small motion causing my muscles to protest. I plant my feet on the carpet and push to stand. A sharp pain rushes through my feet. I suddenly recall the red water emptying into the shower drain last night. Sitting back down, I examine my soles. Several large splinters are embedded in the skin.

I have tweezers in the drawer to the left of the sink, but that means having to make it to the bathroom. Five feet. There are only five feet between where I sit and the drawer. I have to cross a distance less than the average height of an adult, but with my aching muscles and the splinters in my feet, it might as well be a week-long trek.

Cocking my head, I examine the state of the shards of wood. I might be able to pull a couple of the larger ones out with my fingers, but I will certainly need the tweezers for the smaller ones. I grasp the largest one and give it a gentle tug—nothing but a small sting. I bend to get a better look as I tug again. I inhale sharply through my teeth, "Fuck," I whisper to myself. My skin has started healing around the splinters, holding them in place. It is my own damn fault for not noticing last night. I give it a stronger pull, and my fingers slip off the sliver of wood.

"Dammit!" There is no getting around it. I have to man up and get the tweezers.

I debate crawling, but instead put my heels on the floor and use my nightstand to help steady myself as I stand and begin my arduous journey to the bathroom sink. I almost fall as I shift my weight to my right side. Pain darts from my ankle and up the side of my calf, causing visions of kicked doors and awkward landings to flash in my brain.

"I am such a fucking idiot," I mutter to myself as I hobble slowly to the bathroom.

I clear my throat again as I reach the sink and pull out the tweezers, sit down on the closed toilet, and begin drawing the splinters out. Most of them demand wiggling and fierce tugging to break open the skin, freeing the wood from my feet. There is more blood than I expected, so I rinse them under the bathtub faucet. I savor the feeling of the warm water running over my freshly de-splintered feet. I put a bandage on a couple of gashes that are still bleeding and throw on the first clean lounge pants and t-shirt I find.

My face fills with heat as I look myself over in the mirror on my way out of the bathroom. On my neck, right below my jaw, is a smearing of purple, blue, and brownish gray. There is also a deep red line across the front of my throat that fades out in either direction.

I grasp my neck. For a moment, I feel the burn of the cord. My breathing begins to quicken with panic, and as it does, there is a shuddering feeling in my chest. I lay my head on the cool granite of the countertop and take a few slow, even breaths.

I've learned my lesson. Next time, I will be successful. Next time, I will do something painless, something that is guaranteed to work.

My feet still sting as I walk, and I have a bit of a limp from what I think is a sprained ankle, but I can at least move about the room now. I'm careful to avoid stepping on any more splinters as I gather up the small bits of wood. The majority of the beam is still intact, or technically, in two pieces. It looks as if it split in the center under the weight of my body, then shattered a bit once it hit the floor

I toss the shards of wood in the bathroom trash and drag each half of the beam to the wall, out of the way. I can't even lift the damn things.

I'm just sore. Yeah. Just sore. I could lift this if I weren't in excruciating pain. Right? If I could get into the garage to get some tools, I might be able to hang it up again.

I scoff. Who am I kidding? I don't know how to do that sort of thing. Dwelling on it is useless. I can't fix it until Marty unlocks the garage door and tells me how, so I will have to wait until Wednesday to do anything about it.

I need to vacuum up any tiny splinters left in the carpet, but it is good enough for now. I need to lie down. Just that small amount of work has me panting from exhaustion.

I shut my blackout curtains, then retreat to my bed. I pull my blankets over my head and stare at nothing. I let the void engulf me. I let myself relive last night, starting from the moment Rylee kissed me on the cheek and ending only when my life almost did.

That girl tore a hole in my chest. She left me bleeding. It doesn't matter that my attempt wasn't successful last night. Whether I am breathing or not, I am dead. Rylee was the spark that gave me life. She was the only light I could hold on to in my perpetual darkness. That light was extinguished as soon as she sliced me open and bled me dry last night.

I can nearly see her in the dim light of my room. Her eyes are bright. Her red hair is reflecting the lights from my computer tower. A knife is in her hand.

I fall asleep to the vision of her rushing at me. No words. Just her, looking into my eyes and smiling while plunging a knife into my chest. God, what a blissful death that would be.

* * *

This time, when I wake up, I'm not greeted by sunshine. I grab my phone and check the time. 10:45 p.m. Shit.

I finally read the text I had noticed this morning, but decided to ignore.

Mom: "Hey, honey. I'm just checking in to make sure you are doing alright. Love you."

I reply, "I'm good. Love you too."

Sent.

Received.

Read.

No reply.

I can't blame her. I didn't really give her anything to respond to. Despite that, I feel like she should have some sort of maternal instinct, signaling to her that I'm not fine. I don't want to have to ask her for help. I just want her to see it. Sense it.

My muscles ache as I sprawl out in bed. I have slept nearly all day, yet I am still exceedingly tired.

Compared to when I first lay back in bed, my room is much darker. Without the blinding sun piercing my window, my headache eases slightly more.

This darkness is a relief, though it is nothing like the comforting darkness I felt yesterday as I began to fade away.

"I wish I were dead," I whisper. My voice is still hoarse,

but admitting it blatantly and hearing it said in my own voice steadies me. It is the only thing I am certain of now. It is the only thing grounding me. I *will* die. Soon.

I stare into the darkness and imagine what my afterlife might be like as I drift into sleep again.

* * *

I sink into my plush computer chair and close my eyes. My spot. My safety. My distraction. It feels a bit odd to sit here this early on a Sunday morning, but at least I have somewhere to be other than my bed.

A chime from my speakers announces a new Discourse notification. Without lifting my head, I open my eyes and nudge my mouse to get my monitor out of sleep mode.

Sure enough, as if he sensed my arrival, Rex sent me a message. I knew better than to assume it would be Rylee.

Q-Rex: How was graduation? You never got back online on Friday. Or yesterday. You good?

Gr8_nate: Best day of my life.

Q-Rex is typing...

Q-Rex: That good, huh?

Gr8_nate: It was great, Rex, absolutely fantastic! I lost the perfect girl. My parents abandoned me. I made a fool of myself crying my heart out on the front steps of my school. I want to die, but at least I now have a piece of paper that says I completed the most basic education I can receive.

I hold down the backspace key and instead send:

Gr8_nate: It was just fine.

Beep-boop-whoop. Beep-boop-whoop.

I take a deep, quivering breath and put on my wireless

headset.

"What's up, Rex?" I say, my hoarse voice surprising me.

"You spent a whole two minutes typing out a message, but only said, 'It was just fine.'" His voice is a bit deeper than my own and has an oddly calming quality. "Now, what were you *really* going to say?"

I pause and take a deep breath. "Rylee broke up with me."

"Oh, fuck, man. I'm sorry. I know you have been worrying about it since she is moving to New York, but I thought the two of you were endgame."

"For a long time, I thought so too. I don't remember my life before her. She has always been here. I imagined she would always be here. Now it's like an organ I needed to survive is failing. I can only wither away and slowly die because my body no longer works the way it should. Not without her."

Rex doesn't respond. Shit. I'm being weird. This is why people don't like me. I am too dramatic, and I don't know when to shut the hell up.

I hear a deep inhale and then, "Maybe it is a good thing. If she has always been there, this is an opportunity for you to learn to live without her and learn who you are as Nate, not just as *Rylee's boyfriend.* It is hard to separate from people we think we have to keep in our lives, but sometimes you like yourself more without them."

I know exactly what I plan to say to him, but if he is going to let me sit and stew in my anxiety, thinking I said something stupid, I can do the same to him. It is my turn to be silent for too long.

He is right, though. I don't know who I am without her. I don't know who I am at all. I am Nate. I like computer games, anime, a girl named Rylee, and whatever my parents don't.

Well, that's not entirely true. They liked Rylee. The only reason I know her is because we were forced together as children by both our fathers. It was the one thing I was doing right in my father's eyes. I was set to be with a beautiful girl from a successful family for the rest of my life. The problem is that she is living up to her parents' expectations. Not exactly in the way they had initially planned for her, but she will be successful. There is no doubt in any of our minds about that. But me? I am a failure.

My thoughts are halted by Rex clearing his throat on the other end of the call. Shit. I got lost in my head too long. He must think I am an idiot.

"I know this probably isn't the best time," Rex said, interrupting my train of thought again, "but have you been on *R.O.B.* today?"

"Uh. No, why?"

"I was kicked from the guild."

"Wait, what? Hold on a sec."

I double-click the shortcut for the game launcher.

Dominic created *Slayers of the Rich* five years ago. I was one of the founding members, along with Liam and Hayden. Aside from us, we picked up about 50 other players while questing or completing raids. We only invited great players.

The game launcher pops up on the screen, and I sign in.

I invited Rex to the guild about three years ago after the *Abyss of Celephopodus* raid. It is hard as hell to find a decent support player, and Rex was the best I had ever played with. Still is. Despite being a glass cannon, with Rex's strategic dealing of buffs and heals, I rarely go down when I play with him.

I select my main from the character selection screen and tap the '*g*' to pull up the guild manager.

"Fuck. No guild affiliation." I let out a huff of laughter. Of course. "Rex, I'm sorry. This is my fault."

Ever the positive one, he says, "Don't worry about it. We will find another guild to join."

I sigh as I focus on that word. *We.* Just Rex and me. And it hits me—

"I think you might be my only friend now, Rex. Those guys I formed the guild with were friends of Rylee's. They probably only dealt with me because she did. Now that Rylee isn't in my life, I guess they aren't either."

"Look, I don't know those guys very well, but you don't need them. You have me, and I'm the best." He lets out a sarcastic chuckle. "So, have you been sobbing theatrically all night? You sound like shit."

"Nah. Rylee gave me a parting gift. Mono."

"Well, shit."

"Alright, hop on, you bastard."

Rex only snickers, but a pop-up notification at the bottom of my screen reads: Q-Rex is now playing *Realm of Battlecraft.*

* * *

After only a couple of hours, Rex has to get off for work. I'm not sure what he does, but I know he only works a couple of hours at a time and gets to work at home. To me, it sounds like he has life figured out. Rex and I are the same age, but he is miles ahead of everyone I know. Especially me.

I take Rex logging off as a sign to step away from my desk as well.

With a groan, I stretch my arms, roll my shoulders, and walk toward my bedroom door. I try to ignore the split beam in the corner of my vision.

I find a cup of ramen in the pantry and pop it in the microwave. The kitchen is usually filled with healthy foods—fresh, organic ingredients that take planning and a certain amount of skill to prepare. Mom must have asked Grace to pick up this junk so I wouldn't starve while they were gone. Well, at least for the first three or four days, anyway.

I dig through the pantry and find a bag of very expensive-looking potato chips. I snag my ramen from the microwave and three canned colas from the fridge, then make my way back to my desk. Each step on the stairs sends a sharp pain through my feet and a throbbing sensation through my right ankle. I manage to limp to my chair and pull up the legs of my pants. I compare my ankles, and the right one is about twice the size of the left one. "Fuck!"

If I have to go to the hospital and spend this lousy summer in a cast, I'll jump off the damn Tobin Bridge.

I feel a buzz in my head and a laugh rising in my throat.

"When will I stop getting shat on? It is one thing after another." I rest my forehead in my palms, the laugh finally busting through along with tears. "I am such a fucking loser. I got dumped. I lost all my friends. My parents couldn't even wait until after my birthday and graduation to go on their European excursion."

I lean my head on my desk and let the tears wash away the overwhelming hopelessness. It feels good to cry, give in to my self-pity, and wallow in it.

Once the tears slow, I lift my head, wipe my eyes, and prop my foot on a crate.

As I recline my chair and grab my ramen, I bring *Total Iron Philosopher* up on MakiRoll.

Three episodes in, and I am over halfway done with the bag of chips.

Two more episodes, and I toss the empty bag aside and reach for the leftover cake.

Another three episodes, and I am wishing I had more soda.

Beep-boop-whoop. Beep-boop-whoop.

I pause the show and pop on my headset.

"Hey, Rex. Already done with work for the day?"

"Uh, yeah, but what do you mean by 'already'? I got into a flow and was at it for six hours."

Has it been that long? "Huh. I guess time is just zipping by for me today."

"I checked my Discourse notifications after finishing my project and noticed you were active, so I thought I'd check in. How are you doing?" Rex asks, sounding almost concerned.

"I'm doing alright." I lie.

"What have you been up to?"

"Well, since we got off *R.O.B.*, I have just been snacking and watching anime." For six hours straight, apparently.

There is a slight pause before Rex says, "Look, I don't blame you for having a couple of days to feel sorry for yourself, but maybe tomorrow, try to get out of the house. At least get out of your room for a while. It isn't healthy to stay cooped up."

"Thanks for being concerned, Rex, but I'll be fine." *Once I am dead,* I add silently. "Want to continue our search for a new guild?"

"Sorry, but no. I am going out to meet some friends. I'll be on after, though."

"Alright, I'll talk to you later then." I end the call and shut down Discourse, then switch my status on Fuel from active to invisible. Now, no one can see that I am online.

46

The colas I drank now force me out of my chair and into the bathroom. I bring an empty can with me, rinse it out, and fill it with water from the faucet. I find the first aid kit under the sink and take the cold pack with me to my computer.

I take a sip from my can of water. It tastes metallic with a faint cola flavor. It's sort of gross, but it will do. I rest my leg back on the crate below my desk, shake up the cold pack, and place it on my swollen ankle. I sure as hell will not walk down those stairs again today.

My room is already mostly dark, but I shut off the desk lamp and put on my headphones so I can be completely absorbed by the game. I scroll through my Fuel library to find a game to play. I need to massacre something. Punching zombies in the face sounds cathartic. I launch *Zombicide*, and that is where I stay, enveloped in a different world until I can't keep my eyes open. I pop a couple more pain relievers and crawl into bed.

* * *

I open my eyes to see that my room isn't flooded with light like it usually is—finally, a rainy day. My head is still aching and my neck is sore, but thankfully, my ankle doesn't look as swollen today.

I grab some cereal from the kitchen and retreat to the dim sanctuary of my bedroom. By the time I make it back up the stairs, I feel out of breath. I need to take it easy again today. Rex can scold me all he wants.

When my computer boots up, I realize my background is still a picture of Rylee. I feel a hole open in my chest. I can't have her staring at me every time I get on my computer. After all, I'm

47

on this computer to escape the pain *she* is putting me through.

I start up Discourse, and while I'm waiting for it to update, I browse my photos to find a new background, one without Rylee.

Rylee and I at the movies. No. Rylee and I at the beach. No. Rylee and I at the gaming convention. No. Rylee's tits. Fuck no.

What do you do with nudes after a break-up? I'm certainly not making it my background. I could keep them, you know, for reasons.

That feels creepy.

Maybe, in some backward way, holding on to these could help me get over her. If she comes back to me, I'll still have them. If I really have to move on, I can delete them and fully let her go but maybe not until after I get a new girlfriend. That could be years.

The next picture has me adjusting my pants, Rylee sucking on my cock. This was taken in the hotel the night of the gaming convention. We had fun with our phone cameras that night. The next picture is of her on top of me.

I've looked at these pictures a thousand times. Still, they never fail to get me fired up. I pull my dick through the slit in my boxers and jerk off as I click through the photos.

Rylee kneeling on the bed naked. Rylee on top of me. Rylee making that cute little face she always made before she came. Rylee throwing her head back, moaning my name.

My name. I will never hear my name on her lips again. I will never again feel her skin against mine. I will never feel the tickle of her hair against my face while we cuddle. The realization hits me like a stone and softens me. I want to hold her, touch her, kiss her. There is no way to push away this longing I feel.

Tears begin streaming from my eyes and onto my dick, limp and still poking out of my shorts. I let out a sob, my lungs aching as I do. Through the tears, I move all the pictures of Rylee to a separate folder and title it 'Just in case'.

I select a fan art illustration from *Moonglow Orchards* as my new desktop background.

Beep-boop-whoop. Beep-boop-whoop.

I quickly wipe my eyes, shove my dick back into my boxers, and throw on my headset.

I sniff. "Hey, man. What's up?" I sniff again.

"I didn't realize mono gives you the sniffles." Rex chuckles.

"It doesn't. Hey, theoretically, what do you do with nudes after a break-up?" I ask.

"Theoretically, out of respect for my ex, I would get rid of them. Is that how you've been spending your morning? Crying over old pictures of Rylee?" Rex says in a feigned sympathetic tone.

I pause. "Something like that. Let's run some dungeons and try to find a new guild or at least a decent tank."

"Sounds good, but..."

"I know, I know. You have to get off in a few hours to work."

Rex chuckles. "You know me so well."

* * *

The next couple of days pass as if I'm living the same day over again. Wake up. Play *R.O.B.* with Rex. Eat a microwaveable lunch. Watch anime. Order dinner. Play a game where I beat the shit out of things for a while. Then, I finish up my day gaming with Rex again.

The only variations to my day are what I choose to microwave for lunch, what anime I want to watch, and what I feel like killing— zombies, aliens, or cannibals.

At least once a day, Rex spews some wisdom about how I am only hurting myself by sitting at home all day. He tells me I need fresh air, sunshine, and fun in the *real* world.

I am not progressing, but I am content. Having a routine is calming. Reassuring. I always have my games to keep me going. I can visit new worlds, save damsels, manage a successful business, or even live a completely simulated life if I want. I can do anything or be anyone, all while never leaving my room. Maybe in one of these lives, I'll be happy. Maybe in one of these worlds, I won't be worthless.

5

Marty

I wake up on Wednesday morning to find that my headache is finally gone. Glancing in the mirror, I see the marks on my neck have faded. It looks more like an oddly placed hickey than a bruise from an awkwardly constructed noose.

Marty will be coming today. He can fix the beam, and the last reminder of my failure will be gone. I feel a bit excited. I can forget about the incident and move on to greater matters, like the new *Edgeplanets* game or my inevitable demise.

I throw on a pair of my cargoes, an old t-shirt, and sneakers, then set out to the kitchen to get my usual breakfast. Instead of taking it back to my room, I sit on a stool by the kitchen island. While finishing my second bowl of cereal, Marty appears at the shed.

"Hey, Marty!" I shout as I head out the back door.

"Hey, Nate," he says, sounding a bit tired.

He is a short, swarthy man with leathery skin from years working in the sun. It makes him appear much older than he is. He brushes his dark, sweat-soaked hair off his forehead and glances toward me as he continues to drag the lawn equipment out of the shed.

He smiles cheerfully at me as I get closer to him. His smile dulls a bit as he glances at the splotch of discolored skin on my neck, but he says nothing. I'm just glad to be looked upon by a friendly face for the first time in days.

"I could use your help with something." I pause for a moment. My ears begin to feel hot. I compulsively twirl the loose thread on the hem of my shirt. "The beam in my room fell. I could use your help fixing it. If you have the time, that is."

"I'd be happy to help you with that, but I have a lot to do here today and only a handful of hours blocked out on my schedule to work on your house."

"What if I help you? I'll do anything I can." Anything to get that fucking thing off my floor.

He smiled at me. It was a small, sympathetic smile I had seen a thousand times before. The smile that says, *Poor little rich boy. He can't do anything himself.* "That sounds good. Show me what I have to work with."

* * *

Marty clicks his tongue, examining the remains of the beam.

"Can we fix it?" I ask.

"You said it fell. The damn thing is in two pieces," he says, gesturing to the ruptured beam at our feet.

More tentatively this time, I ask, "Can we fix it?"

"No, but we can rebuild it." He points to the side of the beam closest to me. "Grab that piece. Let's load these in my truck. Then we can go to the hardware store to get what we need."

I do as he asks, relieved that I can pick up the beam today. I snort out a small laugh; I suppose I was just sore.

I hoist myself up into the passenger seat of his truck and prepare myself for the inevitable small talk I will have to engage in during the drive. I've known Marty all my life. I have probably had more pleasant conversations with him than with my father. It won't be too hard to speak to him now.

"Do I want to know why the beam was in two pieces on your floor?" My chest tightens. Shit. Right out of the gate, he asks me a question I do not want to answer. But it is only natural for him to ask. He is helping me after all. But shouldn't there be a no-questions-asked policy for hired help?

"I was just being dumb." It wasn't entirely a lie.

"Were you fooling around with that girlfriend of yours?" He asks, wagging his finger at the mark on my neck.

I pause for a moment, unsure of how to answer his question. If I tell him Rylee broke up with me, I could have someone else to talk to about it, but he will most likely ask how I got this bruise if it wasn't from her.

To my relief, or possibly dismay, he continued, "I had to fix a beam in your parents' room once. They tried to hang a— never mind. You don't want to hear about that." He chuckles. "The point is that I just had to rehang that beam. In your case, we have to build a new one from scratch."

I try to shut out the thought of my parents hanging a sex swing in their room. "How do we do that?"

"Well, the beam isn't contributing to the room's structure. It's decorative. Since it doesn't have to be strong, it is crafted from four pieces of thin wood rather than one solid piece, as structural beams are. We need to buy four pieces of lumber. Nail them together, stain it, and hang it. The existing mounting blocks aren't damaged, so we can reuse those." He explains.

"It is easier than it sounds. I have the measurements already, and aside from the lumber and wood stain, everything we need is in the shed."

We move swiftly through the hardware store. I jump in front of Marty at the checkout counter and purchase the supplies with some of the money my father sent to my account, and we are quickly on our way back to the house.

"How would you usually purchase all this? Does my dad leave you some money for repairs or something?" I ask.

"I usually use my company credit card and send an invoice to the client."

"Oh, alright." It's good I jumped in front of him before he could whip out his company card. It would be best to avoid my father finding out about this by receiving a random invoice.

We sit quietly for a moment, but then he asks. "Is there a reason why you insisted on paying, Nate?"

"It is my fault it's broken, so fixing it should come out of my wallet."

"You are a good kid. Your parents should appreciate you more." He remarked.

I try to keep my face expressionless and say nothing. I can't confess to him that I think the same thing every damn day. But I am stunned. No one has recognized how my father treats me, at least they have never spoken of it. Maybe it is more evident to others than I thought. For the first time since Rylee broke up with me, I feel seen. I felt like I wasn't alone. We spent the rest of the drive in silence, but it was comfortable, unlike the awkward silence of car rides with my parents.

* * *

When we arrive at the house, we immediately get to work. Aside from holding the pieces of wood together and keeping the beam in place as Marty drills it in, I'm not much help.

I am learning a lot, though. I suppose it is common for sons to help their fathers with projects and learn to use tools, but that was never an option for me. Marty is taking the time to explain everything he is doing as he is doing it. He also lets me attach the last two cuts of timber myself.

Our project is complete, but Marty still has plenty of yard work to do, and as promised, I will assist him the best I can. He instructs me to mow the lawn while he performs more intricate tasks, including trimming the hedges and edging the driveway.

I've never had to do work like this before. The exertion makes me feel alive, and seeing the results of my effort is satisfying. I feel capable of doing something *real* for the first time in my life. For the first time, I feel like I improved something.

I walk with Marty as he heads out the back gate.

"Thank you," I say, "you have no idea how much I needed this."

"Oh, no, I could tell. You looked like an ass swinging that hammer, but after I showed you the right way to do it, you were a pro."

"That's not exactly what I meant, although I am thankful for that too. I needed to do something to wake myself up. This helped."

"I understand, Nate. You are welcome," he says as he climbs into his truck. "I usually work alone. It was nice having company for once. See you later, kid." He gives me a small wave as he begins to pull out of the driveway. He puts on his brakes, "Oh, and I won't tell your parents about the beam." He winks and drives off.

I stand on my front lawn and admire the results of my and Marty's hard work. It looks the same as every time Marty leaves, but this time, I appreciate the work he put into it because I put in some work too. The manicured lawn feels like an accomplishment.

It's lunchtime. I decide to microwave a cup of tonkotsu ramen and retreat to my room to jump back into my usual daily routine.

As I enter my room, I glance up at the freshly constructed beam. Aside from the color looking more vibrant than the other beams, you can't tell that it isn't the same four pieces of wood that were hanging in this spot a few days ago.

I wonder if it is apparent that I am not the same as I was a few days ago. I've fallen and splintered. Maybe I can be repaired too.

* * *

"All these guilds are dog shit," Rex says, sounding annoyed.

"Maybe we are just too picky. It's not like we are *R.O.B.* gods, and every guild out there should want us," I joke. "The next time one of us gets a guild invite, we need to accept it and test them out for a week or two."

"Ugh. I know," he asserts, sounding even more irritated.

"You good, man?"

"I'm fine. I'm just on..." Rex stops for a moment before continuing. "I'm on the outs with a friend right now."

"Do you need to talk about it?" Whatever it is has really got him in a mood.

"No, but speaking of friends, have you gone out at all since graduation?"

"As a matter of fact, you asshole, yes, I have." I sound a little too proud of myself, but even talking to someone is a feat for me, so I can be proud of myself for this.

"Oh? Tell me about it." Why does he sound like he is laying a trap for me?

"This morning, I was helping our handyman, Marty, with a project. We needed some lumber, so we went to the hardware store."

I hear a soft laugh coming from the other side of the Discourse call. "So, you are telling me you ran an errand with someone who was being paid by your family the entire time you were with him?"

I didn't think about it that way. He probably felt like he *had* to let me help him. I was just a burden. In all likelihood, I made his work more difficult for him.

"Yes, I suppose that is what I am telling you."

"That doesn't count, Nate."

I can tell from the judgment in his tone that he is tired of my hermit bullshit. But he is right. I'm pathetic and need to get out of the damn house more.

"If you are so worried about my social life, Rex, maybe we should meet up at Spawnpoint and grab some coffee. You said you live in Boston, too, right?"

Rex lets out a long sigh. "Yes, but I've told you before that I don't mix my gaming friends with my real life. I prefer staying anonymous online, which is why I have never told you my name."

"Right. Let's get back to the game."

I truly am alone. My only companionship is on this screen; my only friend is someone I have never met in the real world.

6

Not Alone

With the new *Edgeplanets* game and the *R.O.B.* update both launching today, Rex and I have a difficult decision to make.

"I don't want to risk any spoilers." Rex whines, "I wish I could just play both at the same time."

"That would be amazing, but unfortunately, we can't make copies of ourselves; we aren't ninjas in an anime," I joke, "and I doubt either of us has the processing power to run both games at the same time, anyway."

Rex chuckles and suggests, "Let's install *Edgeplanets* first, then we download the *R.O.B.* update. It is bound to take forever. We can play *Edgeplanets* while waiting for it to install."

"That's a great idea." Why didn't I think of that? It's so obvious.

Rex might bitch a lot, but he is a strategic thinker, which can come in handy since it is one of the many attributes I lack.

I bitch a lot, *and* I am stupid.

I log into Fuel to buy the new game and start the download. Rex does the same.

"My download should be done in about 10 minutes," I say.

"Mine will be done in about 12."

Rex is silent for a moment, then finally lets out a sigh. "I am sorry for what I said yesterday, you know, about how your time with Marty didn't count as having a social life. The important thing is that you're not isolating yourself anymore. You left your house. That's a good thing. I was being a dick yesterday."

"Oh. It's alright," I say, even though what he said kept me up half the night reexamining all the friendships I have ever had.

"I'm glad you said that. It's been bothering me since I logged off yesterday." He confesses.

"You know, I really enjoyed doing the yard work. I don't know if it was the movement, sunshine, or something else, but I felt pretty good afterward."

"I know what you mean. If I go more than two days without running, boxing, or lifting weights, I feel unnerved and edgy. The exertion settles my mind. I'm glad you found something that makes you feel better. Maybe you should keep doing it."

"Maybe I should." I run the tip of my thumb over my chin, pondering if Marty would agree to let me work with him again.

"Anyway," Rex continues, "I won't be able to stay on for as long as I normally do. I have plans with a friend this afternoon, so I need to start my work a bit early."

"That's cool." Not cool, Rex! What happened to *no spoilers!*? How can you avoid spoilers if you skip out early on release day? "Do you have something thrilling planned for the afternoon?"

"Nothing major, just some shopping and dinner." He says.

"Sounds fun." I lie; I really hate going shopping.

"Eh. Not exactly. I am not into shopping. I am just going because she likes to shop. I give her my honest opinion about the clothes she tries on; she appreciates that."

59

"Rex, you keep saying you don't have a girlfriend, but that sounds like a typical afternoon for a man in a committed relationship," I joke.

"Maybe to you, but I view this relationship a bit differently." He laughs, "She and I are only friends, and that is perfectly fine with me. Promise."

"Whatever you say," I'm not buying it. "This is the same girl you are always hanging out with, right?"

"My game's done!" Rex says, sounding relieved to change the subject.

A notification pops up on my screen saying my game is ready to play.

"Mine too. Let's get started." I crack my knuckles and roll my shoulders. I will let him change the subject for now. I can easily work my way back to it when he comes back later.

The next two hours are well spent, murking irradiated cannibals.

* * *

It has been ten minutes since Rex left, yet I'm still scrolling through my library of games trying to decide what to play.

Before he logged off, we resolved that neither of us would continue *Edgeplanets* without the other. I also reluctantly agreed to hold off on playing the *R.O.B.* update until he is back online. So here I am, unsure of how to spend my afternoon.

I tap my foot and look around my room, trying to find something to keep me occupied. Something to distract me and keep my mind from swirling into a pit of despair, like being flushed down a metaphorical toilet of depression.

Fuck. I'm a dork. Spending all this time by myself is making me weird. The gurgling of my stomach interrupts my thoughts. Next task acquired: obtain sustenance. I put my palm on my forehead. What is wrong with me?

I rummage through all the kitchen cabinets and the pantry; I only find one cup of noodles remaining. I am also out of cola. I have no snacks. Everything in the freezer and the pantry requires preparation. I let out a long sigh and microwave my final instant ramen. I guess I will starve.

While I sip the broth from my soup, I sit back at my desk and continue scrolling through my games. Something mellow might be nice for a change, like a life simulator or a civilization management game.

Sim Life? Mm, no. *Terracraft?* That one is *always* tempting, but no. Of course! *Moonglow Orchards.*

It's one of those games where, if you play it, the gatekeepers of gaming say you aren't a *real gamer.* Well, fuck them. If I want to grow trees with fruit that glows at night, make friends with the eclectic villagers, and break a spell cast by The Wizard of the Woods, I will. I do what I want, goddammit.

I start installing the game, and my stomach growls at me again. One cup of noodles just won't cut it.

I have plenty of time to kill before Rex returns from his *not*-date. I may as well run to the store. I could easily get groceries delivered, but I should get out of the house. I look at the time: 2:53 p.m. If I throw on some clothes quickly and run to the stop, I should make it in time to catch the 3:00 p.m. bus.

I used to ride the same bus to come home after school. If Rylee and I had plans after our classes, I would take the 6:45 p.m. bus to make it home by dinner time.

I grab the first pair of pants I see on the floor. My thoughts linger on those afternoons walking along the harbor with

Rylee's hand in mine. Her thumb grazes over the back of my hand. The breeze tousles her amber hair. The fall sunset casts an orange glow on her cool skin.

She always preferred a pink sunset. She said it complemented her skin tone better. I think she looks beautiful in any light. I push my yearning aside. Focus on what you are doing, Nate. If I can't concentrate, I will not catch the bus.

Despite my lack of focus, I make it to the stop just in time to see the bus arrive. I'm surprised to find that jogging here made me sweat. I suppose I have not been very active lately. I feel a slight shudder in my chest as I catch my breath and find a seat.

There are only a few people on the bus already, so I can choose almost any seat I like. If I sit in the front, it will feel like everyone is staring at the back of my head, but I will be able to get off the bus quickly when my stop arrives. If I sit in the back, I will not be stared at, but I will have a long walk down the aisle. If I walk too slowly down the aisle, I will feel like I am holding everyone else up. If I walk too quickly, I will seem like a bumbling freak.

I opt for a seat at the front.

I take the city's transit often, so I am familiar with the different types of weirdos you might encounter on any given bus. I usually find them entertaining, as long as they don't try to convert me to their religion or buy their teeth.

Today, I feel like one of those bus lurkers. Not a single person looks at me for more than a second while the bus makes its stops. The majority of people break eye contact immediately. I check my reflection in the window to see if there is anything on my face. No. As far as I can tell, my face is clean. I dip my head down to sniff myself discreetly. I don't smell shower fresh, but my deodorant is doing its job.

I begin playing the text-based RPG on my phone. I simply won't look at anyone. Problem solved. If I am distracted, I can forget that the other commuters exist. My chest blotches bright red as I avoid looking up. A tense feeling arises at the nape of my neck, as if everyone's gaze is slowly burning a hole through it. No matter how hard I try to block out the rest of the world, I cannot escape it wholly.

My stop finally comes, and my choice of seat is finally validated. I hop off the bus as swiftly as I can. Since I was the only person getting off at the store, nobody else had to wait for me. The bus barely even had to stop.

The relief I feel getting off the bus is short-lived. I swallow hard as I walk through the automatic doors and into the fluorescent hell that awaits.

The best way to do this is to do it quickly. I grab a shopping cart and rush down the aisles. I drop cups of ramen, bags of chips, and packs of cola in the cart. I slow my pace to browse the snack aisle.

Do I want chocolate chip or peanut butter cookies? My stomach tightens when I hear someone walk up behind me. I turn slightly to glance at them from the corner of my eye. They twist at the same time, pretending to examine the crackers. I know I am in their way.

Just make a decision, Nate! My upper lip begins to sweat. They are waiting on me. My breath and my heartbeat quicken. This is ridiculous. I frantically glance between the two, striving to make my verdict. I snatch both off the shelf.

Indecision. Yet another of my undesirable traits. I can't begin to list all the things I have missed out on or bought too many of because of it. I can't decide which cookies I want, so I buy both. I can't decide which college to enroll in, so frozen in indecision,

I let the enrollment period pass me by.

On my way to the self-checkout kiosks, I notice a mini-fridge blocked by an elderly man who seems to be comparing toasters. I bounce up and down on my toes, pretending to be considering which blender to buy.

Get out of the way. Get out of the way. I want to get out of this damn store. Move. Move. Move.

I almost decide to skip it and go to the check-out, but after what feels like an eternity, the man finally chooses a four-slice toaster and moves along. Without even looking at the box, I snag the mini-fridge off the shelf and add it to my cart.

I scan my groceries as quickly as I can. I didn't consider how I would get all this home when I was plucking it from the shelves. I load up my arms with five canvas grocery bags and place the two 24-packs of cola on top of the mini-fridge box.

It is heavy and awkward, but I manage to make it to the bus stop. There is a weirdo sitting on the bench. You can always tell who the creeps are. His face looks vacant and stern. He is glaring up from below his eyebrows with piercing, red eyes.

I still have five minutes before the bus arrives. My choices are to sit on the bench and risk a five-minute tirade about the end of humanity or stand here and hold all this shit.

I attempt to adjust the bags on my left arm and nearly drop the fridge. Fuck it. I'll sit with the creep.

I sit down on the bench, squished up against the left armrest, as far away from the guy as possible. As expected, he turns toward me, smiles, and says, "Hello."

I give him a small nod and gaze down at my groceries sitting on my lap. I can sense him staring at me. I glance at him from the corner of my eye, and I see he isn't looking at me but at my shopping bags. He doesn't look like someone hard up for food, but I hold my bags a bit tighter anyway. He looks clean, but he has a peculiar scent I can't quite place.

He glances up at my face, notices I am looking at him, and says, "Sorry, man. I saw those peanut butter cookies, and it is taking all the self-control I have not to snatch 'em and gobble 'em up."

My first instinct is to clutch my snacks even tighter, but I finally recognize what I am smelling and laugh. "No worries. I bought too much junk anyway." I take the cookies out of the shopping bag and slide them across the bench to him.

He immediately rips open the box. "You are a lifesaver, my friend!"

This isn't a bus lurker; he is just stoned and hankering for cookies. I smile at him and give him a more friendly nod this time. He digs into the cookies and extends the container to me, offering me some. I have only eaten cereal and one cup of ramen today, so I grab three cookies and scarf them down.

The bus arrives just as I finish my last cookie. I choose to take a seat in the front and place the fridge and food in the seat beside me. The pothead slides into the seat behind me and taps my shoulder. "You're," he draws out the word and pauses.

"Nate," I say, at the same time he says, "off."

"I'm off?" Maybe I misjudged him. He is stoned *and* a bus nut.

"Yeah. You. Are. Off," he says in staccato, tipping his head side to side with each word.

"Care to elaborate?" Why am I even entertaining this guy right now?

"You look like you are lost, or maybe deep in thought. No. That's not it. You look annoyed to the depths of your soul. You are eternally pissed off."

"What kind of shit are you on, man?" What normal person says something like that to a stranger?

He puts up both his palms in resignation. "Whoa! I meant no offense, Cookie Man. All I mean to say is, what's troubling you, friend?"

Friend? I can feel the bewilderment revealed on my face.

He smiles broadly and says, "Hey, you can form an expression other than resting douche-bag face! I'm so glad." He chuckles. "I'm just messing with you. You looked like you needed someone to ruffle you up."

Resting douche-bag face, huh? Is that what is keeping people away from me? Am I showing the emptiness I feel internally on the outside? Do I really look so miserable?

"My girlfriend of three years broke up with me a few days ago. I guess you could say I am pissed off."

I turn around to face him. He looks genuinely concerned. How can someone care this much about someone they've just met?

"That really sucks. The good news is that you are young."

I examine his face. "You're like, maybe two years older than me," I say, but he ignores me.

"You have years ahead of you to find new love and make a life." He gets a little closer and whispers, "I believe in you, Cookie Man."

The bus stops at an apartment building, and the stranger stands up. "This is my stop." Like an older brother I never had, he tousles my hair and says, "Stay out of trouble, little dude."

I scoff, "I'm taller than you."

"Only on the outside, my friend," he says with a wink.

In stunned silence, I watch him bound down the bus steps. What the fuck was that?

* * *

This is the first time I have ever bought food for myself. Granted, I didn't earn the money I used to buy it. But, honestly, my father didn't *earn* it either. This is the first time I went to the store and bought exactly what I wanted. No expensive instant ramen that tastes like crap. No fancy bags of potato chips that taste exactly like the stuff you can find in any vending machine.

I chose these things. Me. I had control over it. Not Father. Not my mom. Me.

I step back and admire the pantry full of food. Microwavable bowls of macaroni and cheese, cup ramen, canned spaghetti and meatballs, a massive box of microwave popcorn, peanut butter, bread, and three boxes of General Munch cereal are all neatly lined up on the shelves.

I make my way to the freezer to put away my pizza pockets and corndogs, then put the jelly, ketchup, and one case of cola in the fridge. I grab the remaining two grocery bags, the second case of cola, and the mini fridge and bring them to my room. I plug the fridge in next to my desk and load it up with the second case of soda.

The fridge makes a perfect shelf for three bags of chips, chocolate chip cookies, and two boxes of little cakes: one vanilla and one chocolate.

Now that I am set for breakfast, lunch, and snacks for the next couple of weeks, it is time to order dinner.

I decide to order a large pizza with sausage, pepperoni, and banana peppers. I eat half of it and watch four episodes of *Assault on Gigantor* before Rex finally sends me a message on Discourse.

"Hey, man, ready to kick some skakt ass?" he says, referring to our quest to slay 20 bat-dog hybrids in *Edgeplanets 2*.

I switch my audio to my headset and call him.

"I was starting to think you weren't going to get online. I figured you went back to her place. God, you deserve it after going shopping with her."

A huff comes from the other side of the call. "First of all, I told you it is not like that with her. Second of all, I'm not *owed* anything if I decide to do something that I don't enjoy simply because my friend does. Just spending time with her is enough for me. Don't be an ass."

Things must not have gone well tonight. "Okay. Okay. You're right. I'm sorry. How about we play some *R.O.B.*?" I suggest, not wanting to piss him off anymore.

"Nah. I have already tried to get on. The server is maxed, and the line to get in is insane. We should try again tomorrow."

"Sounds good to me. Let's kick some skakt ass."

I watch what I say very carefully for the rest of the evening.

* * *

Today, Rex and I finally get into our usual server in *R.O.B.* As tempted as we are to try out the new Gorgonotaur race (the result of a gorgon and a minotaur getting their freak on), we decide to play the storyline update with our mains first.

"Nate!" I hear someone yelling from downstairs.

I gasp, "What the fuck? Someone is in my house."

"What?" Rex asks in an unnecessary whisper.

"Nate! Get your ass down here!"

"Wait, I know that voice. Hold up, Rex. I'll be right back." I remove my headset and rush out of my bedroom and down the stairs.

"What's wrong, Grace?" I say to our housekeeper, whom I found in the kitchen.

She is a tall woman with a mix of silver and golden blonde hair. Her eyes are kind with small lines between her brows, which suggest she has had a lot to worry about. She has a slight accent that I can't place. It's the kind of blended accent that sounds like she was raised in the States but by parents who were not.

"What's wrong, Nate, is that all I see in this trash can is takeout containers, pizza boxes, empty chip bags, cola cans, and crushed ramen cups."

I stare at her blankly, not knowing what to say.

She continues, "All I see in the fridge and pantry is junk!"

I continue to stare at her. I'm used to verbal lashings. The best thing I can do is stay quiet and let it pass.

"Hasn't your mother taught you how to cook?" She asks, exasperated.

"My mom can't cook. When she tries to, we end up spitting it out and ordering takeout instead." I continue, "We have a chef prepare our weekday meals and usually order takeout on Saturday and Sunday unless my mother wants to try her hand at domesticity or I'm told to *fend for myself*."

"I didn't realize." Her tone changes completely. "Oh!" she says, like she remembered something she meant to say. "I'm sorry about Rylee. I know the two of you have been inseparable since you were toddlers."

"How do you know about that? I haven't even told my parents."

"Well, the Dunwall's maid told Marty, who told me." She shrugs. "The rumors are true. The help talks." She chuckles, attempting to lighten the mood.

This fucking aristocratic life. Everyone is connected in one way or another. There is no fucking privacy.

"It's fine," I avoid eye contact, so she can't tell how *not fine* I am.

She seems to sense that I don't want to talk about it and changes the subject. "Your parents cut my visits to only once a week for the next couple of months since they won't be home. Not that it really makes a difference. Your parents are gone so often that you are the only person who makes any sort of mess in this house." She winks, "But don't tell your parents that." She lets out a small, warm giggle. "Does your room need cleaning?"

"No, I can keep up with it myself." I don't like the idea of anyone seeing the absolute mess my room is turning into.

"Okay. What are some of your favorite foods?"

The question catches me off guard, but I respond, "Um. I really like roasted chicken, chocolate chip cookies, and mac and cheese."

"Good to know," she says. "I'm sorry I disturbed you. Go back to whatever it is you were doing."

"See you later," I say, and head back to my room.

* * *

"Hey, sorry about that, man. I was talking to our housekeeper."

"Wow. A housekeeper. You and I live vastly different lives, Nate," Rex laughs.

"She knew about Rylee breaking up with me. If she knows, everyone knows."

"So what if they do?"

I suppose he is right. Everyone was bound to find out

70

eventually. It was inevitable.

Rex continues, "This is the first time you have talked about her in a few days. How are you doing?" Rex responds softly, as if he is talking to someone in hospice.

"I'm fine. I'll be okay. Rylee is always on my mind, but even more so today. It's Friday. She always streams on Friday nights. I am fighting the urge to watch her. I know I shouldn't. Seeing her would just fuck with my head. But I want to see her smile again. I want to hear her voice." I stop myself before I can go on about her too long. I'm such a downer. It's no wonder I drive everyone away. "I'm sorry. I'm so annoying, rambling on about her."

"I'm the one who asked. You don't have to apologize. I've been a bit of a dick lately. I'm sorry if I made you feel like you couldn't talk about her."

"You've been fine, Rex. I always annoy people. You can ask me to shut up if you need to," I laugh.

Rex takes in a sharp breath. "This might come as a shock to you, but I care about you. I'm sure there are others, too."

"Maybe."

"Your housekeeper and Marty both seem like they care."

"Maybe."

Regardless, more people hate me than care for me. Dominic, Hayden, Liam, Ashe, Mom, Father, and Rylee are, at *best*, neutral toward me. The only people who care for me are a housekeeper, a handyman, and a stranger.

"Tell me everything about Rylee. Tell me everything you have been holding in."

"Are you sure? You won't tell me anything about yourself, but you are fine with me spilling my guts?"

"Just tell me what you feel comfortable with. I've been in a

71

place where I felt like I was alone, too, so I know that holding all this in isn't good. I made that mistake in the past. I know better now. Just trust me and learn from my mistakes."

"Okay." I know I need to vent and let some of this go. If this stranger is the only person I can talk to, so be it.

I take a deep, steady breath and begin. "I first met Rylee when I was a little kid. She was the first friend I ever had." I tell Rex the story of Rylee and me, from the first memory I have of her to the words she spat at me to push me away.

We never get back to playing the game.

I carry on about her for an hour. Rex sits and listens. He only speaks up to tell me he thinks Liam is a dick.

By the time I am done, I am sobbing. I haven't felt this vulnerable since the first time Rylee saw me naked. I've sliced myself open and let my blood pour out.

"Do you feel better?" Rex asks

I sniff. "I do. I didn't realize how much I needed to get out."

"Well, we talked all the way through her stream, so you don't have to deal with that temptation anymore. You aren't a burden to me, Nate. You are my friend."

7

Cheers

"I have a date," Rex said timidly. He must feel awkward, or even guilty, for bringing it up because of my recent breakup.

"Ooh, you have a date." My feelings of jealousy and vicarious happiness duel within me. "Is it with that one girl? You know, the one you are always hanging out with."

"Sierra? No, it isn't Sierra," he says, sounding a bit irritated.

Sierra. At least I know the girl's name now, but—is Rex a fuckboy? I know next to nothing about him. He seems too respectful to be a player. Not the point. "So, you need to get off early?"

"No, I am not even getting on this morning. I just jumped into the chat to let you know. I will be on this afternoon, though," Rex clarifies.

"What the hell kind of date are you going on at 9:00 a.m. on a Saturday?"

"We are going to the farmer's market and probably having ice cream after."

"Oh, wow. Well—"

He interjects, "And please don't give your opinion on it

because the plans were my idea and I am nervous enough already."

Rex is on edge this morning. Maybe I *should* keep my snarky comments to myself. "It sounds like a great first date, if that is what this girl is into."

Rex lets out a long sigh. "I think it is. This is my first date in years," he says.

"In years? You are 19. How has it been *years* since you've been on a date?"

"Well, it's been two years. Actually, maybe I've never been on a date. I don't want to get into that right now, but I had some things happen when I first started dating that made me decide to swear it off. Anyway, I have to go. Talk to you later."

"Later. Good luck, man." I log off Discourse and tap my foot a couple of times.

Now what?

* * *

After two episodes of *Rice Balls Basket* and three bowls of cereal, I launch *Moonglow Orchards*. I play for three in-game days, hoping to get into it, but I can't. I scroll through my game library, but nothing grabs my attention.

I slump in my chair and rest my head on the desk. How am I supposed to distract myself by playing these damn games if I don't feel like playing anything without Rex?

I am just getting into a funk. Since I started hoarding snacks and drinks in my room, there hasn't been much reason to leave it. It would be nice to stretch my legs a bit.

I stand from my chair, straining my muscles as I do. I'm sore. It has been quite a while since I stood for longer than the time it takes to get from my desk to the bathroom and back to my computer again.

I get up from my chair and walk down the hall, not sure what I am planning to do. There are many rooms in this house that I never go into. I have no reason to. I stop in front of my parents' bedroom and pause with my hand halfway to the doorknob. I suddenly recall what Marty said about having to repair the beam in their bedroom.

Yeah, I'm going to be scarred for life if I snoop around in there.

I turn and continue down the hall. There are two guest rooms—one with a king-sized bed and the other with a queen and a bunk bed. I used to spend the night in the latter room when I had sleepovers as a kid.

Those days of dares and stupid pranks are long behind me. I'm expected to be grown already, but I'm still that kid. Lost. Self-conscious. Foolish. Now, these rooms are only used when we have family visiting or if my mom and father are having a fight, and they sleep in separate rooms for a while.

I don't want a marriage like that. I want a marriage where I can look forward to holding my wife in my arms each night. A marriage where arguments last just a few minutes and are easily shrugged off, not fights that end up in separations that span multiple days.

The final room on this floor is used as storage, but it also contains a linen closet and the stairs to the attic. That room always gave me the creeps. This house is updated and aesthetically fine; it's a bit basic, but something about the age of the house, combined with the emptiness of the upstairs rooms, gives me chills.

I decide to explore downstairs. I have lived in this house my entire life, yet I am hardly familiar with the rooms. I know what they all are, but I rarely venture into them. I learned from a young age that if I sneak off to my room, I am usually forgotten about pretty quickly, so I hide out most of the time I am home.

Today, I am going to explore the whole damn thing.

I start by familiarizing myself with the kitchen. Copper pots and pans, usually only used by a hired chef, hang from hooks above the island. I find metal and ceramic bowls and a fancy mixer in the cabinet to the left of the oven. The other cabinets are filled with everything one would expect in a kitchen. There is a shelf devoted to spices, another with three different types of sugar, two different types of flour, baking soda, baking powder, and corn starch.

Why am I finding something so mundane to be so interesting? Am I *that* starved for stimulation?

I stop in front of the stove and ponder the many dials. It is a gas-powered stove. I've never had to turn it on. I saw my mom light it, one of the few times I have seen her attempt to cook us a meal.

Tick tick tick tick tick. No flame.

I've heard of accidents—horrible balls of fire that consume houses and the people inside because someone misused one of these stoves. I push in the dial and turn it again.

Woosh. A blue flame dances under the grate.

If I felt like leaving my parents without a home, I would consider having one of those *accidents* myself. I turn the dial to the max and wiggle my fingers through the fire. I resent them, but I'm not unfeeling enough to do that to them. Or to put Marty and Grace out of their jobs.

Another option would be to turn on the gas, let the gas fill the house, and go to sleep. Maybe making my death look like an accident would be best. Nobody could blame them. I could spare them the embarrassment of having a son who would rather kill himself than live the life they created for him.

I turn off the burner.

* * *

I decide to partake in another first today. I'm going to piss in a bathroom I have never pissed in.

Exciting.

Directly below the stairs, next to the kitchen, there is a half-bathroom. My mother always says not to go in there because it is for *the staff,* as if we can't shit in the same toilet as the maid.

It's much smaller than what I am used to. I only have to take a single step to get from the toilet to the sink. I wash my hands, but there is no towel. With dripping hands, I squat down to look for one in the cabinet below the sink. I find a single, dusty towel, but something behind it grabs my attention. A wicker box nearly big enough to hold a pair of shoes. The lid is askew, as if whatever is in it doesn't quite fit.

I dry my hands and toss the towel on the ring. I reach into the cabinet to pull out this mystery box. It is probably potpourri or fancy hand soaps or something, but it is still a box I've never seen before, and the whole point of my little adventure is to discover new things, so—

I clear my throat, feeling silly about getting worked up about something so mundane. I lift the lid.

Oh, this isn't mundane. No, not mundane at all.

In the box, I find prescription bottles, a shit ton of them.

I pick them up and read the labels one by one: Sarah Whims, oxycodone 5 mg. Sarah Florence Whims clonazepam 2 mg.

Nathan Whims III, methylphenidate 60 mg. Sarah F. Whims, clonazepam 1 mg. Sarah Whims, zolpidem ER 7.5 mg. Sarah F. Whims, oxycodone 3.5 mg. Nathan Graham Whims III, dextroamphetamine-amphetamine 15mg.

I drop the bottles back inside the box and place it under the sink exactly as I found it, which wasn't difficult to do as it fit perfectly in the only dustless area in the cabinet. I position the lid on top, perfectly awry.

* * *

I press my toes hard into the plush rug in the entryway, pacing back and forth. Each time I turn, a new question arises.

Is my mother addicted? How does she get these pills? Why does she have prescriptions in my name? When did this start? *Why* did this start? Does anyone else know? Does my father know? Has Grace seen my mom's stash while cleaning the room?

The dust. No, Grace couldn't know. Something tells me the staff aren't *actually* allowed to use that toilet.

If she doesn't know, it's probably not public knowledge. When the maids find a juicy bit of gossip, everyone knows sooner or later. I would have already heard about it if that were the case.

My mother could kill herself. I knew already that she drinks too much, but *this*? This is scary. This is *reckless*. Is she using all that wine to wash down some medley of psychotropics?

I feel the familiar buzz in my head. My chest begins to tighten, and my breath quickens. Before my body completely falls into panic, I take a seat on the Victorian-style armchair in the parlor. I hug my knees to my chest and take three calming breaths.

There is nothing I can do about it right now. Even when she returns home, there is no point in confronting her about what I found. She will give me that girlish smile and say, "I don't know what you are talking about, dear." And prance away as if my world isn't reeling.

I sit back in the chair, which is made to look good, but not provide comfort. I need to put it out of my mind. There is nothing I can do about it. I just need a distraction. I glance around at the room full of equally uncomfortable furniture. A chair identical to the one I am in sits to my right on the other side of a small end table. Across from these chairs is a couch that seats three people. Finally, a chaise is placed against the wall under the window that looks out on the front lawn. They are all the same boring beige shade with reddish-brown wooden legs.

I am usually only called in here to welcome visiting family members or when my mother hosts holiday parties. Otherwise, I try to avoid this room; it is usually where my father is if he is not in his office.

I've never noticed that the legs on the seating match the other wooden furniture perfectly. The tea table, end tables, and liquor cabinet are all the same wood. Hell, even the sideboard in the entryway is the same shade of brown; I'll call the hue: *elegant shit*.

The room is boring. Basic. Safe. Just like Father.

Even the art hanging on the walls is unexciting. The paintings don't conjure a poignant response and require no interpretation or thought. Maybe that is by design. Perhaps, a lack of emotion is preferred in a room made for pleasant smiles and small talk.

I tip back my head and stare at the ceiling. The swirling

thoughts pelt me again as soon as I stop distracting myself. I let out a long groan, which turns into a guttural scream. I am in agony.

I rise quickly from the chair, trying to summon any vitality that remains in my bones. The motion only tweaks my ankle, and I fall back into the chair. I need to feel something more. I need more than to feel empty and alone. I need *something* to help.

I wonder if my mother's issues are just adaptations. This could be her way of managing the facade she wears daily to appease my father. She has to have some way to cope. This isn't really her. This *can't* really be her.

I look to the chaise on the other side of the room, remembering all the mornings I would find my mom asleep, or possibly passed out, there.

I have always known my mother was unhappy with her life. But these drinks have made it possible for her to wake up next to my father for 20 years.

Maybe some drinks could help me through this god awful summer.

It takes one glance at the lock on the liquor cabinet to know this will be an easy pick.

I grab two metal skewers from the kitchen and get to work. I insert one of them into the bottom of the lock and another into the round, top portion of the lock. I slowly and carefully wiggle and turn them until...*click.*

Yes! Years of lock-picking chests in dungeons pay off. Granted, those are video games, and this is a basic lock only meant to keep out children, but it is still a win.

I look through the bottles. The liquid inside them varies in color. Some are brown, some are clear, some are colors you wouldn't expect, like green or red. Clear sounds like a good starting point. Most have brand names that I can't pronounce, but I recognize the vodka and grab the whole bottle.

In the kitchen, I find a tall, skinny glass from the cabinet with the less fancy drinkware and fill it with ice. I examine a steel, double-sided shot glass I found in the liquor cabinet and contemplate which end I should use. I've seen the bartender at the Christmas parties pour the liquor for my half-strength drink into the smaller side, so I think this time I should go all in. I fill the larger side with the liquor, dump it into the glass, and top it with cola.

"Cheers to a life of loneliness and misery.", I say, and down the drink. The entire thing.

I make the same drink again, allowing the shot glass to overflow just a bit as I do. I clutch the bottle in one hand, my glass in the other, and retreat to the darkness of my room.

* * *

Beep boop whoop. Beep boop whoop.

"Reeeeeeex! Hey man, how did your date go?"

"Um. My date was okay. They were a bit shy, but I see some potential. I'll probably ask them out again."

"I am soooo happy for you, bro. You are awesome. I bet they are awesome too-*hiccup*- they just need time to heat up. Warm up or whatever."

"You seem chipper. And uncharacteristically energetic." Rex lets out a long sigh. "Nate. Are you drunk?"

"Bitch, I might be."

"You-" Rex clears his throat. "Did something happen while I was away?"

I let out an embarrassingly boyish giggle and slur out, "You would *not* believe what I found today."

"I think it is pretty obvious what you found today. It was in a bottle, right?"

"Yes!" Not the bottle he is thinking of, but, technically, he is correct.

There is another sigh on the other end of the call. "Jesus Christ."

"I got bored after you left. I decided to poke around in the rooms I don't go into much." I say, poking at the air.

"And one of those rooms had a stash of booze, huh?"

"Ugh. Let me finish telling you about my life-changing journey," I whine.

"Life-changing?" Rex scoffs.

I ignore him. "I was looking around the house and I had to piss, so I went to the closest bathroom, one I had never used before."

Rex interrupts, "I can't believe there are so many bathrooms in your house that there was one you hadn't used."

I clear my throat, ignoring his comment. "I looked in the cabinet and found a box. I *thought* I was going to find fancy-shaped bars of hand soap or something." I pause for dramatic effect.

"So, what *did* you find?" Rex says, sounding more annoyed than interested.

"But alas! It was not hand soap." I pause again.

"And it was?" Rex asks, sounding frustrated and impatient.

I take a breath, trying to keep the true weight of what I found from sounding in my voice.

"There were pills in the box. Some were in bottles with my mother's name, and others had my name on them," I say in a more serious tone than I had been using. "I think my mother is addicted. So, yeah, what I found was in a bottle. Many bottles."

I hear Rex's breath catch. Then, he is quiet. He is quiet for so long, I feel like he might have walked away.

I can't take the silence anymore. My anxiety takes over. I begin to well up with tears as I say, "I just wish I could tell Rylee. She always knew what to say when my parents were being shitty. She would hold me and twirl my hair in her fingers." I break into a full sob. "God, I miss her. I love her so much. I am worthless." Through the flood of tears, I whisper, "*Worthless* without her."

After what feels like an eternity, Rex responds. "That is why you shouldn't be drinking right now. If your mother is addicted, it could be a hereditary trait. And drinking while you are already emotional is not a good idea."

My stomach twists. Rex is disappointed in me. He is the only person I have now, and he's disappointed in me.

"Reeeex. Are you mad at me?" I whine out.

I hear a light sniff on the other side of the call. "Nate, I have lost too many people in stupid, *stupid* ways before. You are my friend. I don't want to lose you, too. Please, Nate. Please, don't go down this path."

"Okay. I won't drink anymore." Today, anyway. "I'm going to sleep."

"I'll call you in the morning," Rex says before hanging up.

* * *

Before I open my eyes, I am hit with a throbbing headache and the urge to hurl. I roll off my bed and crawl in the dark to the toilet. The moment I feel the cool porcelain under my fingers, my stomach wretches and spills everything I had eaten before and during my little party for one.

I rest my head on the toilet seat, but immediately lift it and begin vomiting again. And again. And again, until it is nothing but a singeing yellow liquid.

My vomiting finally subsides. I place my head on the toilet seat again, snag some toilet paper to clean my face, and slump to the floor.

* * *

I am awoken again by the sun shining through the bathroom window. Groaning, I sit up from the uncomfortable position I found myself in on the tile floor. The soft light pierces my eyes. I click my tongue a few times in my dry, sticky mouth. God, I need to brush my teeth. The taste of bile is still coating my cheeks, and my breath is rancid.

So this is a hangover. I expected worse. This is only half as bad as waking up the morning after—I clear my mind of the thought. And, instead, try to recollect the previous night.

As I recall the things I said, my face heats with shame. The way I was acting, I was a complete idiot. I learned something very private about my mother, and the first thing I did was tell someone whom I've never met. And the way I was crying about Rylee— I cover my face with my hands. I am so embarrassed.

I place my hands on the tiles in front of me and hoist myself into a standing position. As soon as I am up, I am hit with queasiness. The headache is rough, and I feel exhausted, but I can deal with it. It is what I deserve to feel like.

I lean on the sink and stare at my reflection in the mirror. Bloodshot eyes, dry lips, and the indentation of the tile floor on my cheek. Yup. I look as shitty as I expected, but still not nearly as bad as *that* morning.

I brush my teeth and turn the shower on. I hadn't noticed until I slipped off my shirt that there was a crust of vomit right below the collar. And my lounge pants—I can smell them two feet away. God, I am disgusting. When did I last bathe?

Through my exhaustion, I manage to take a shower, get dressed, and make two cups of ramen. Ah, yes, this is what I needed. Comforting, salty, and full of carbs—perfection. I inhale the steam rising from the foam cup and lean back in my desk chair.

I have about two hours to kill before Rex usually gets online, so that means I have two hours until I receive the inevitable big brother-style lecture. He and I are the same age, but he acts all high and mighty, like he knows so much about life. I can't stand to admit it, but that guy is the only person who seems to care for me right now. I could at least hear him out.

Beep-boop-whoop. Beep-boop-whoop.

Well, speak of the motherfucking devil.

"You're up early," I say in place of a proper hello. I'm dreading the verbal lashing he surely has planned for me. I might as well launch right into a different subject rather than leave the air open.

Rex, sounding tired, only says, "I couldn't sleep."

"Oh, that sucks. I'm sorry, man," I say, trying to sound sympathetic.

"Yeah."

And the air is open. Why bother calling if he doesn't have anything to say? Maybe he isn't the person who should be talking. I planned what I would say to him in the shower earlier. I might as well be the first to speak and get it over with.

"I'm sorry, Rex. I was a mess yesterday. I made a bad call. An impulsive, dangerous call. I shouldn't have pushed my problems onto you. I shouldn't have burdened you with my issues."

"When will you get it through your head? Next to Sierra, you are my *best friend*." Rex's tone was earnest, verging on pleading. "And that is why you scared me yesterday. It kept me up all night. I *care* about you. You can tell me all about your problems; they aren't a burden to me. Let me help you."

"I'm sorry I worried you." The words were automatic, but genuine. I have been foolish. He isn't just a familiar voice in my headset. He is a person. A friend I have bonded with over hours of quests, raids, and dungeons. I have told him everything for the past two years, and he has offered me honesty and wisdom in return. If he weren't the same age as me, I would have felt like he was the older brother I never had.

"It's okay. Just—" He pauses as if checking what he is about to say, or possibly the way he is saying it, "make smart choices."

* * *

Apart from taking a break for an after-lunch nap, Rex stayed online with me all day. He claimed to have no pressing work and no plans with friends, but I know Rex; he is never online all day. He finds other things to do because he wants "balance" in his life. He made the time for me. Spending all his time with me was his choice.

Someone chose *me*.

8

Hopeless

It is Wednesday, and as usual, Marty is pulling into the driveway at 8:00 a.m. sharp. I was dressed and ready to meet him at the gate to the backyard by 7:55.

He grinned at me. "Don't tell me you broke something else." He snorted.

He seems to be in a decent mood this morning. Good.

My heart thumps in my chest, and I resist the urge to fidget. I have never felt comfortable asking for things. Especially when I know I am burdening someone.

"No, I was up and just thought I'd say good morning."

"Well, alright. Good morning, Nate," he says as he makes his way to the shed.

"Good morning," I say again, like a fucking doofus.

I turn on my heel and begin walking back to the house.

I would just be an encumbrance. I'm not wanted or needed here. I should just go back upstairs and do what I am truly good at: playing games and being a leech on my parents' backs.

As I start to open the door, I hear footsteps coming up behind me.

"I hate to ask, but do you mind if I use your can?"

"My...can. Oh, yeah. Come on in."

I point him to the "staff" toilet. Thank God I used it first, so he wouldn't have to scrounge for a hand towel and find my mother's stash in the process. If I were in some random rich person's house, I wouldn't be able to resist the urge to rummage through the cabinets, regardless of whether they employed me or not.

I stood in the kitchen, not knowing if I should give him space or wait around for him. I end up just shuffling my feet. I hear the toilet flush and immediately feel like a fucking weirdo. Who waits for someone outside a private bathroom? I'm a creep. What if he thinks I was worried about him stealing or snooping or something?

The faucet on the bathroom sink turns off. I turn to the fridge and rifle through the shelves as if I were looking for my breakfast. Casual. Not creepy. Calm. Not accusatory.

"Thanks for that, Nate. I usually don't like to ask to use the client's toilet, but the one at the gas station down the road is disgusting."

Says the man, who has dirt all over his clothes. Though I know the restroom he is talking about, it should be condemned. The whole convenience store should be condemned.

I grab two bottles of water off the top shelf and look at him over my shoulder. "No, problem."

Marty stands there for a moment. "It seemed like you needed something earlier. If you need anything done, don't be afraid to ask. That's what your parents are paying me for." He glances at the two waters in my hands and back at my face.

"I know."

He lingers a second longer, nods, then walks to the back door.

This is my last chance to ask without seeming like an awkward basket case.

I almost turn and leave, but the familiar motion and feeling remind me of all the other times I had needed to say something and hadn't been able to get a word out. How many times could my life have been altered if I just said what I needed to say?

Maybe Rylee would still be with me. Maybe I wouldn't be friendless. Maybe I would have a family that loved me.

Without another thought, I blurt out, "Can I help you with the yard work?" *Blurt* is an understatement. I just damn near screamed at him.

"You don't need to be afraid to ask me that either." He smiles at me and waves me over. I hand him one of the bottles of water, and we walk out the back door.

* * *

Unlike last week, we have plenty of time to complete the yard work since it was the only task to complete today. There is no wreckage from some clumsy attempt to end my life to clean up. When I finally kill myself, I will keep it clean.

Also, unlike last time, we don't initially split the tasks. Marty takes time to teach me how to use each tool: the weed eater, edger, hedge trimmer—apparently, I, a typical child of privilege, have somehow been using a fucking rake wrong. There are no callouses on my hands and no dirt under my fingernails. I'm a spoiled waste of air and space.

Once I proved I could use each tool without maiming myself or causing an absolute mess of things, I was allowed to take a go at the whole yard.

I put my earbuds in, turn on some lo-fi, and switch on the

tool. As soon as I feel it buzzing in my hand, my mind goes quiet. My inner monologue quits spewing racing thoughts of "what if" and self-deprecating comments. All I feel is a flow of calm energy from my brain to my heart, from my heart to my hands, and from my hands to the tools.

I work in straight, paced lines. Learning the required speed and movement of each tool takes some trial and error. Eventually, using the tools begins to feel natural, as if my arms have extended to form blades or whirring wires.

I am clipping the final stray branch from a hedge when Marty taps my shoulder. I snap from my trance and tear out my headphones.

"Hey, bud. I didn't mean to startle you. It looks like we are all set."

I pull my phone from my pocket to check the time. "How the hell has it been two hours?"

"I get like that too when I work," Marty admitted with a wide smile. "I still have some time to spare. Why don't we sit and chat a while?"

I run inside the house and grab two more bottles of water from the fridge. We sit on the steps to the back deck and stare out at the yard in silence.

As I wipe the sweat off my forehead, I feel that same sense of accomplishment I did the time before. I feel lifted. Fulfilled. I did this. I did something real.

Marty patted my back, "Not bad for your first time."

"Maybe I am a natural," I joke.

"Now I wouldn't go that far," he lets out a boisterous laugh. "But not too shabby."

"It's better than sitting at my computer for 16 hours a day." I shrug. Why the fuck did I just say that?

"I heard about you and your girlfriend, Nate. I also heard you aren't going to college *or* working for your dad."

I look down at my feet. I alternate tapping them. Right. Left. Right. Left. Left. Right. Not knowing what to say, I shrug again.

"Are you okay?" In the corner of my eye, I see Marty's gruff demeanor soften slightly, "What are you going to do?"

I turn my head and look at his face. A look of genuine concern was fixed there. It made me want to be honest with him. "I don't know what to do."

"I'll tell you what you can do. You can help me with your yard again next week. And if you need anything before then, call me." He hands me his business card. "Be good to yourself, Nate."

With that, Marty rose and began walking back to his truck.

"Next week," I respond without standing.

It takes me thirty minutes to find the motivation to stand up and go inside.

* * *

After a quick shower, a cup of ramen, a bowl of cereal, and two cookies, I don't find myself back at my computer. I find myself staring at the liquor cabinet.

When Marty asked me what I planned to do, something snapped in me. Like a physical string was plucked in my brain. The feelings of accomplishment and satisfaction I gained from working in the yard immediately switched to a sinking feeling in my gut.

What am I doing? What am I doing? What am I doing?

Rex would be pissed at me. Marty would be upset with me, too.

Knowing full well it is a bad idea, I reach for the bottle of tequila.

I'll be more responsible this time. I can have a couple of drinks without getting completely sloshed. I'll just drink a bit to take the edge off. Rex won't be able to tell at all.

To be safe, I won't take the whole bottle with me. I find a tiny funnel and a flask in a small cedar box. I open the bottle and take a sniff. Jesus. I put the cap back on and reached for the vodka instead. I fill the flask to the brim. I don't really remember how much I drank the other night, but I doubt I will get entirely blasted from a single flask. I slip it in my pocket and walk to the kitchen.

Shoved to the back of what I would call the miscellaneous cabinet, I find a plastic cup from our most recent family vacation and our only trip to the New Jersey boardwalk. The image on the cup was faded, but I could make out the year printed on it. I haven't been on vacation with my parents since I was 12 years old. I'm sure they won't bring home a souvenir as cheap as this one from their fancy European excursion.

I make my way to my desk, brooding as I walk. I doubt they will bring me a souvenir from this trip at all. If they do, it will be something I hate. Something generic and halfhearted. Something they bought three of, just in case they forgot to pick up a souvenir for a friend or business partner. Or their offspring.

I sit down at my computer and pour the vodka into the cup. I count 1—2—3: a three-second pour and a can of cola. I will remember that. I will keep track this time. I take a sip directly from the flask and follow it with a hefty swig of my vodka and cola.

I immediately feel a warming sensation, which calms my

anxiety a bit. I crack my knuckles. This is the perfect time to play *Summons of Allegiance.*

I play round after round, losing most of them. And sip drink after drink.

Beep-boop-whoop. Beep-boop-whoop.

"What the fuck are you doing? That game makes you toxic."

"Well, hello to you, too, Rex. Are you done with your work for today?" I totally sound sober. I can pull this off.

"Eh. Yes and no. The job isn't complete, but my inspiration has run out for now. Feel like running a couple of dungeons with our Gorgonotaurs?"

"Most certainly." I will keep the talking to a minimum. There is no way he will know. "Let's run 'em up!"

"Are you drinking again, Nate?"

Already? Rex is a fucking wizard.

"No, why do you think that?"

"Well, you are slurring and talking ridiculously loud," he says. "You are also being abnormally enthusiastic, which is exactly what you did last time."

I end the call. I know where this is going. I don't need to get preached at right now. I feel good. I don't need some high and mighty prick telling me I am an idiot. I don't need someone else making me feel like shit.

I shut down discourse and turn my online status to invisible on Fuel. I move to relaunch *Summons of Allegiance*, but end up staring at the screen instead.

Marty's words pop into my head. *Be good to yourself.*

I don't fucking deserve to be good to myself. I pour more vodka into my only half-empty third drink and top it off with more cola. I deserve to be dead.

I launch *Sim Life* and make a character with my likeness. I take extra time on my dimensions: gaunt with hauntingly long arms. I make him appear unsettling, as if he is just slightly inhuman. In the box that says, "Name," I type, "Nate Whimless". I move Nate into a small room with no windows or doors.

I save my game and add a fireplace to the room. I leave Nate standing next to the fire as it begins to spread.

I watch as Nate panics and burns to death. I watch as the reaper appears and drags Nate to Hell.

I load my previous save and add a toaster.

I command Nate to use the toaster until it breaks and then fix it. I watch as he gets electrocuted to death. I watch as the reaper appears and drags Nate to Hell.

I load my previous save. This time, I build a pool outside and tell Nate to go for a swim. I switch back to build mode and construct a fence around the perimeter of the water.

I pour another drink and watch as Nate treads water. Slowly, he runs out of energy and drowns. I watch as the reaper appears with floaties on and drags Nate down to Davy Jones' locker.

I let out a long exhale and notice my walls moving. I retrieve my phone from my pocket and open my text messages from Rylee.

I should have known a long time ago that the end was coming. I rest my head on the cold desk and scroll through our old messages. She only sent one-word responses in the final week of our relationship. She hadn't initiated any conversation through text for the past month and a half. Three months ago, she started sending "love you" instead of "I love you." The signs were all there.

I am such a fool.

I close my eyes and feel the total weight of my failures wash over me. I'm alone. Alone. Alone. And I treated my only friend like shit this afternoon. Remembering the hint of disappointment in Rex's voice churns my stomach.

I lunge for the small trash can beside my desk and violently hurl up my lunch. Without thinking, I grab the nearest drink to get the taste of bile out of my throat. I taste the strong flavor of vodka and immediately vomit again.

"Fuck," I groan, tears forcing their way from my ducts.

I retch again, and only a frothy yellow liquid comes this time. My tongue is coated in an acidic, disgusting tang. I heave again, but nothing comes up. My stomach feels like it is trying to leave my body.

I sway my way to the bathroom, where I rinse out my mouth. I brace my hands on the bathroom sink and glare at my miserable reflection. I look paler than I did before. I look sallow and sick. Despite the hours upon hours of sleep I have been getting, I look absolutely exhausted. I am awash in feelings of shame and can't bear to look at myself for another minute.

I somehow manage to get to my desk chair again. I am relieved to see that Rex is still online. I start a private call with him. It takes all of a second or him to answer.

"Rex, I am so sorry. I suck. I suck. I—"

"I was so worried about you," Rex says in a soft voice I had never heard from him. "I know you are having a hard time. I know you are lost. But I am here. Please." His tone sounds desperate, "Please don't destroy yourself, Nate."

"I'm sorry."

"Stop! Stop apologizing. Stop doing this to yourself."

"Rex, I don't know what to do." Tears begin streaming from my eyes, snot running from my nose. "I don't want to feel this. I don't want to feel anything. I am no one and nothing. I'm unwanted by everyone: Rylee, my parents, and even you. You won't meet me. I'm utterly alone. I just want it all to fucking end." I take a deep breath, trying to halt my crying.

"Nate," he stammers. "I am your friend. I know I have been weird about meeting in person. I know you've been hurting. I—we— maybe we can meet soon. I don't know. I, um, I need to go. Just go to bed. Don't do anything stupid. Life gets better. I know it is hard to see now, but it is the truth."

"How do you know that?" I ask a bit more aggressively than intended.

"Because it got better for me. Goodnight, Nate. Just go to bed. Call me in the morning. Please."

"I will. Bye." I say, and immediately hear the beep of Rex leaving the call.

I stare at the screen blankly for a few moments as I try to consider the implications of what Rex said.

It got better for me.

Has Rex wanted to kill himself before? Has he tried?

I keep my word to him and crawl into bed.

* * *

I have stayed in bed almost all day. To keep Rex from worrying, I sent him a message telling him I was hungover and just wanted to lie around and watch TV. It was a lie. I stayed in bed, yes, but I wasn't hungover. I had avoided that with my puking session the night before and the liter of water I downed before I passed out. The part about watching TV was also a lie. I spent my time taking short naps and staring at the ceiling, the fan, and the cobweb, which I didn't realize was in the corner.

I don't want to move. I am disgusted with myself. I'm ashamed. I was so transparent with Rex last night. I laid myself

96

bare. I shredded myself to the bone and handed him my flesh to dissect.

Groaning, I roll over and check the time on my phone; 2:30 in the afternoon. I continue to stare at my phone and watch the minutes pass by. 2:31...2:32...2:33. I'm wasting another day just as I have wasted every moment of my life. 2:34...2:35. A message pops up on my phone. I have almost stopped getting my hopes up that my unread message is from *her*.

Of course, it is from my mother, who is the only person who texts me anymore. "I hopw you r dong well. Lobr you!"

I wonder what she is on now. Wine? Maybe she found a way to get drugs over there?

I roll onto my back again and count the fan's rotations as it whirls around on low speed.

My stomach lets out an audible grumble. I can't be bothered to get up. I can't be bothered to eat. Maybe I can stay here forever. I could let myself starve to death.

I begin picturing shapes in the texture on my ceiling. A dog. A creepy face. Boobs. A pretzel.

I roll onto my stomach, bury my face in my pillow, and scream. I scream and scream until I run out of breath. I scream out of frustration. I scream out of boredom. I scream out of desperation— desperation to go back four years and do it all over again.

I need to go back and spend my high school years figuring out what I want to do. I need to find something to work toward, so I can be worthy of her. So I can be her equal and hold her hand as she walks down the red carpets she is destined for.

My stomach growls again. I ignore it and close my eyes.

* * *

I open my eyes and jump out of bed, run to the bathroom, and pee for what feels like an eternity. I walk back to where my phone was sitting on my bed and look at the time—four hours had gone by while I napped. It's wild how easy it can be to spend nearly an entire day in bed.

My stomach feels hollow as I trudge down stairs in a groggy haze. I peruse the kitchen for something to eat. The shelves are already getting bare. I gently hit my head on the pantry door.

"Ugh! I don't want to go to the store again," I whine. I can make it through today, but I grossly underestimated how much I actually eat.

I manage to scrounge up a makeshift meal of a peanut butter sandwich and microwave macaroni and cheese. Instead of going back to my room immediately, I decide to eat at the island in the kitchen.

I don't feel ready to return to my dark hole yet. The sun is just about to set, and I feel the need to hold onto the sun just a bit longer. I down my food and do something I have seen my mother do many times. I pour a glass of wine from a bottle I found at the back of the pantry. It was one of many, many bottles.

I take my glass to the back patio, where I sit on the plush lounge chair and stare at the pink and orange sunset, just as my mother spends her late afternoons. She usually brings the whole bottle with her.

I inhale deeply and exhale slowly. I sip from my glass and immediately want to spit it out, but I swallow anyway. Another sip has me going back inside and topping it with cola.

Much better. I guzzle a bit and feel a rush of warmth. Like I am wrapped in a hug and floating above the ground. I understand now how my mom can get lost in a bottle every night. It is comforting to drink, and given that she is stuck with my father, I'm sure she could use all the comfort she can get. I return outside and sip on my cola wine until all the sunlight has faded from the sky.

I'm almost ready to face Rex again.

* * *

I wake up to the sound of metallic clanging coming from around the corner of the house. I jolt and quickly stand from the chair. Two mangy-looking cats haul ass across the yard and jump over the privacy fence one after the other.

I rub at my temples, still feeling a bit tipsy from the wine, as I walk to see what caused the noise.

The trash can on the other side of the gate had been knocked over, and two garbage bags had tumbled onto the lawn.

"Those furry little dickheads," I sigh and tug open the gate. I turn the bin upright, and as I bend to pick up one of the bags of trash, a warm gust of wind blows. I hear a slam and click behind me.

"No no no no no." I run to the gate and try to pull it back open. It's locked. I've fucking locked myself out. I try to find a way to open the gate, but I can't see anything in the shadow between houses, away from the street lights. I groan and pat my pocket, expecting to find my phone, but come up empty.

Great. No light. No phone.

I brace my hands on the top of the wooden gate and pull myself up, or try to. God damn, I am weak.

I hoist again, this time pressing my feet into the gate to give myself a boost. I tumble over and land on my back. *Hard.*

Why can't I catch a fucking break? It's either one thing or the other. Never the right thing. Nothing can go right for unfortunate Nate.

I lay motionless and panting for a moment, then I sit up and put my head in my hands. "What am I doing?" I whisper into the night. "What will I do?"

Feeling foolish and clumsy, I stand, dust off my already disgusting clothes, and go back to the patio. I grab my phone and wine glass off the lounge and walk back inside.

I head back to my room, plucking the half-empty wine bottle off the counter on my way.

I shut the door behind me. My room is dim. The glow of my monitor and the lights on my computer tower are the only light sources in the room. My solitude. My dark cave.

I sit at the computer and pour myself some more wine. Rex is online, but I don't care. I switch my status from "away" to "invisible".

I just need to turn off my brain and kill things for a while. I scan through my library of games in search of the most disturbing, violent game I own.

9

Grace

I walk down the stairs to find my mother in the kitchen. Her hair is up in a tall, twisted bun. She is wearing a knee-length dress with a pearl necklace and matching pearl earrings. Her smile is sober and genuine.

"Mm! That smells delicious, Mom!"

"I made your favorite, Sweetie. Ramen and chocolate chip cookies," she says as she begins loading the dishwasher.

"Let me help," I say as I make my way around my mother and take the dish from her hands.

"Aw, you don't have to do that, dear." I give her a smile that says I'd be happy to help. She grins at me, but looks different now. She has dark bags under her eyes. Her hair is out of place, and her teeth are stained red with wine.

I begin to load the dishwasher as she takes a seat at the kitchen island and sips from a cup of coffee.

I hear my father walking in from the hallway. "Sarah, who are you talking to?"

"Morning, Father," I say in a neutral tone.

I pick up the lid to look at the food cooking in the pot. Three electrical cords tied into a hangman's knot are boiling in the broth. My breath catches as I look back at my mother.

"Well, Nate, of course," she quirks her lips in a crooked smile and rolls her eyes as if my father is crazy. She looks even more disheveled now, in a filthy t-shirt and sweatpants, her hair mostly pulled from the neat bun she wore just a moment before.

My father grabs her by the shoulders, dragging her from her seat. "Sarah, you need to stop this madness. He is gone! Stop making this food. Stop playing pretend." He clutches her arms and shakes her as if he can shake her to her senses. "Our boy is gone."

My mother wells with tears, her teeth begin dropping from her mouth between sobs. "Thanks to you." She spits one of her teeth at his face. "He is gone because of *you*," she whispers, scowling at him.

He releases her arms and smacks her across her face. She collapses; as her body hits the floor, it shatters into a thousand pills.

I sit up, sweating and panting. It was just a dream. That's all. Just a weird-ass wine dream. It felt so real. So, so real. I take deep breaths, trying to steady myself.

After about a minute, I finally calm myself and reach for my phone to check the time. Before I can grab it, I hear clanging coming from the kitchen.

I whip my head in the direction of the sound. My breath catches. My heart feels like it has ceased beating entirely.

I take a deep breath and don a new pair of sweatpants and a hoodie. I slip slowly down the stairs, unsure of what I will see or if I am still dreaming.

"Oh, good! You are up! A bit late, don't you think?"

I let out a sigh of relief. "Grace! You scared the shit out of

102

me!"

"Hey! Watch your fucking mouth, young man."

I roll my eyes. Yeah, this is undoubtedly real.

"I have a surprise for you," she says as she plops an entire raw chicken on the counter.

"What the fuck is that?" I ask with a grimace.

She smirks and puts a hand on her hip. "I am going to teach you how to cook."

I scoff, "I beg your pardon."

"Under my instruction, you will season and roast this bird."

I say nothing.

"I will also teach you to make homemade macaroni and cheese."

I say nothing.

"And bake chocolate chip cookies from scratch."

I turn and start walking toward the stairs, but Grace grabs me by the shirt collar like a mother in a black-and-white TV show.

"How do you expect to get a new girl if you can't cook?" Grace crosses her arms and looks at me expectantly.

"I'm not really motivated to find a girlfriend right now. But—"

"But?"

"You have a point, and I am starving," I sigh and roll up my sleeves. "Fine."

"Yes!" Grace pumps her fist like she just had a small victory. "Wash your hands. Tell me everything you already know about cooking."

"Well, I know that is a chicken," I say, pointing one of my freshly washed fingers at the pale chunk of meat and bone on the counter.

Bap!

"Grace, did you just smack me with an empty paper towel roll?"

"I certainly did. And I will do it again if you continue to sass me."

"Ugh. Fine. I played a cooking simulator for a while. Obviously, it wasn't real, but it probably taught me *some* real cooking techniques." I flinch, expecting to get swatted again.

She glares at me. "I'll just figure out what you know as we go. Let's start with the cookies."

Grace showed me the ingredients to use and the correct way to measure them. She demonstrated how to properly crack an egg and sift flour. When it came time for her to teach me about all the different knives found in the kitchen, she gasped when she asked me to grab the chef's knife, and I selected the right one. "You don't know how to measure flour correctly, but you know what the different knives are called?"

"Using the right knife was crucial for getting a high score in the cooking sim—"

Bap!

"Dammit, Grace!"

Bap! Bap!

"Don't cuss at me, boy."

"Yes, Ma'am."

Bap!

"Don't call me Ma'am!"

"Alright, fine. Jesus." I flinch, realizing what I said.

"Don't worry about that one, Nate. I don't give a flying fuck if you 'use the lord's name in vain'," she says while doing air quotes.

I smile, feeling relieved.

"Anyway, back to cutting vegetables."

She teaches me how to shield my fingers while holding the vegetable in place. I chop carrots into thick half-cylinders, quarter an onion, and half a lemon. I stuff all of that in the bird's cavity. I take sprigs of rosemary and thyme, and a few whole sage leaves, and shove them up the bird's ass as well. I spread the remaining carrots at the bottom of the roasting pan.

I chop the same herbs I used for the inside of the bird and mince garlic. I put all of it in cheesecloth and let it simmer for a while in a pot of melted butter.

"Why not just let the herbs float in the butter?" I ask.

"Because we are going to be using this," she says, pulling a giant syringe from a drawer. "We can't have the herbs getting stuck in the needle."

"So we are...?"

She clarifies, "We are injecting this herb-infused butter into the chicken," and gives me an excited, wide-eyed smile. "Now, let's prep this mother clucker."

There's still plenty to do with the chicken while the butter is being infused with the flavor from the herbs.

I pat the chicken dry with paper towels and rub the skin with oil. I use grinders to sprinkle salt and pepper over the surface.

When the butter reached room temperature, I suck it up with the syringe, then shot it into the meat of the bird in multiple different places until the pan of butter was nearly empty. It was at this point that Grace hands me a silicone basting brush and instructed me to coat the skin with the remaining butter.

Grace hands me a glass shaker jar. "Use this!"

The label appears handmade and taped on. Little herbs and flowers are doodled around the name, "Herbes De Provence?"

"Yes! I put this together myself with herbs from my garden."

I give it a sniff. The scent is a fantastic blend of botanicals and zest. I take a second whiff. And there is something else. "It smells a bit like a flower," I say.

"That's the lavender," she says proudly.

"We are cooking with flowers?"

"Trust me! It's going to be great!" She says it so enthusiastically that I can't help but believe her. I sprinkle on a generous helping, then tent aluminum foil over the chicken.

I open the oven door and shove the roasting pan inside.

Grace claps her hands together in excitement, "Now we start the macaroni."

Just as she walked me through the cookies and chicken, she walks me through the process of making the mac and cheese: Boil the pasta, cook the sauce, and prepare the casserole dish. Apparently, you bake *real* mac and cheese.

Grace says it is time to let the skin crisp up, so when it is time to put the macaroni in the oven, I remove the foil from the chicken.

"What do you normally do while your meal is cooking?" I ask Grace.

"Well, sometimes when I cook, I run around the kitchen from start to finish, but for meals like this, where it bakes for a while, I like to play a game with my family. You have board games in your family room, don't you?"

The family room. I haven't been in there in years. "Oh, yeah."

I lead Grace to the family room. Nobody except the family and Grace comes into this room, so it has more character than the other rooms. It exudes my mother's personality. This is where she stores all the junk she picks up while shopping. Trinkets, blown glass sculptures, and toys her parents couldn't afford to buy her as a girl are all displayed on shelves on either side of a large TV. Mom spends a lot of time in here. I suspect she comes in here to indulge in the childhood she never had.

I open the double doors to an ornate, wooden armoire filled with every type of board game and card game you can imagine: city-building games, strategy games, party games, trivia games, and classics like chess and backgammon. There are games in this cabinet that take 10 minutes to play and games that you can play every evening for a week and still not finish. Games are another one of my mom's fascinations. It is one of the few I am interested in, too. She hasn't wanted to play in a long time, though.

"Ooh! This one! This one!" Grace hops excitedly as she snatches up a red box of cards.

Grace settles in on the couch, so I sit in the adjacent chair and shuffle the cards. I kick her ass for two rounds, but then on the third round, Grace seems to have a change in luck.

"Aha! Reverse this, bitch!" She shouts and slams a wild, draw four onto the coffee table.

I protest, "Hey, if I can't cuss at you, you can't cuss at me."

"Game time smack talk is different, bitch."

"Alright then, Fuck you and fuck your draw four!" I shout.

She smiles and says, "Ah! You are catching on!" as she slams down a yellow draw two.

I glare at her.

"You are such a goofy person, Grace. You don't find that puts people off?"

"I used to be worried about it. I used to try to disappear because I thought I would say something stupid or do a dumb dance, and people would think I was weird. I learned it was something to celebrate and embrace when I found Mike, my husband. He has always loved my happy dances and my sense of humor. Now, I get to raise two girls who know it is best to embrace who they are and show the world who they are because we are all only promised this one life. Live it happily and free."

I stay quiet for a moment and let the truth of what she has just said sink into me.

"You seem to enjoy cooking a lot," I say, trying to move the conversation forward.

"I do," she says. "I would never want to do it professionally, but, as far as hobbies are concerned, it is my calling. And I love cooking with others. The best part of my day is when my girls and I put on our matching aprons, turn on some music, and create something scrumptious together. We will play games with my husband while it is in the oven or after dinner. Mike knows not to go into the kitchen when we are cooking. He only gets in our way." She laughs softly with a smile that is so content it makes something sour take root in me.

"Your family is lucky to have you," I say, feeling jealous that I wasn't born into a happy family.

"I'm lucky to have them." She gasps then shouts, "Last card!"

A high-pitched beep comes from the kitchen.

"Fuck!" We both say in unison, but she continues, "Let's finish this round! It won't be ruined in, like, two minutes."

She wins on her next turn.

The food smells amazing. The scent of the cheese, herbs, and vegetables blends into an aroma of sheer comfort. It smells like home. It's a scent I have never known before.

We eat our lunch together. The food tastes just as good as it smells. Maybe even better. The macaroni and cheese is better than I have had in any restaurant. The chicken is juicy with layers of flavor and a crisp skin, which I tear off the meat. I put some macaroni and cheese on the skin, and roll it up like a burrito. Delicious.

Grace tells me she has time to do the dishes before going to her next job. I insist on helping her and shake off a feeling of deja vu.

* * *

It is a weird feeling to have your morning be filled with so much light and laughter, then *BOOM*, it's gone as soon as the front door closes.

Cooking with Grace made me feel like a functional, present human for the first time since graduation. This was the first time I had real *fun* with another person in weeks, and the first time I had truly laughed in months.

Going back to my room feels like giving in to the darkness, and I am not ready for the void after spending all morning with the light that is Grace.

I take my time cleaning up the plates from lunch, trying to hold onto the natural sunlight shining through the windows and French doors in the kitchen.

I scuff my way to the stairs, but as I enter the hall, I am drawn to the shut and locked door to my father's study. What could be so important that he feels the need to keep the doors locked at all times? Why does he never let my mother or me inside without basically having to set an appointment with him beforehand?

I turn the handle to his office door, and as expected, it is locked. I pause. The last time I decided to explore this house, I found something that destroyed me. Who knows what I will find in here if I continue?

Maybe it will finally give me the push I need to end my life.

That is all the motivation I need to track down the metal skewers and try my hand at picking the lock.

It is a more difficult lockpicking job than the liquor cabinet, but eventually, I hear the *click*.

I open the door slowly. The smell of musty cigars and leather greets me. The room is dark. Flipping the ceiling light on feels like I would wake some long slumbering beast, so I carefully walk across the room to flick on the lamp in the corner next to the desk.

I make a slow lap around the room and take in everything. All the covers of architecture magazines he has graced are framed and hung on the wall: seven Boston Architecture Quarterly issues and three Modern American Architecture issues.

Nathan Whims Jr.: A Bostonian Architect on the Rise in New York City.

Nathan Whims Jr: The New Face of Whims' Architecture.

Nathan Whims Jr: A Look into the Life of a Boston Philanthropist and Designer.

I wasn't even mentioned in the article about his life's story.

I take a stroll around the room, taking in every aspect. The last time I had been in here was my 16th birthday; during that discussion, I had just been staring at my wringing hands. I never had the chance to take in the whole room.

This space is dramatically different from the other rooms in the house. The rest of the house is beige and brown, with the occasional green, red, or blue thrown in. It is filled with natural light. It is boring but inviting.

My father's office is dark and ominous. The walls are painted red, the same shade as dried blood. There are two standing lamps and a single desk lamp. The two windows are covered in blackout shades. Fake potted plants sit in the corners of the room.

It is like a burrow. No air. No light. Anything that needs either of those things certainly could not survive here. Perfect for an undead plague rat like my father.

There is a small liquor cabinet, a sideboard with an empty crystal pitcher and matching glasses on top, and an antique filing cabinet that belonged to my grandfather and my great-grandfather before him.

I open the drawers to the filing cabinet one at a time and flip through the files. Each one is devoted to a project and divided into several categories. Current projects are in the top drawer, upcoming projects are in the second drawer, and completed projects are in the third and fourth drawers. He is tech-savvy enough, so he most likely has a digital copy of each on his computer. He has always been the type to hold on to paper copies regardless.

Placed on the far side of the office is the real object of my curiosity, my father's desk, another antique passed from my retch of a grandfather.

To dissuade me from rummaging through his desk, my father would tell me a story about how his father smacked his hands with a steel scale ruler until they bled after he was caught poking through the drawers. Recalling the story now, I feel more curious than ever. What was so private inside Grandfather's desk that it was worth bloodying up his child? Nobody will catch me. The house is mine. Father is an ocean away.

I pause in front of the desk and stare at its neatly organized surface. A leather cup of pens sits on a matching desk mat. There is a lamp, a coaster, and a framed photograph of my father and grandfather at the latter's retirement party. It is the happiest I have ever seen my grandfather look. He appears to be filled with pride and relief. He built a successful firm and passed it on to his extremely talented son.

What if my father is just a product of his environment? Maybe he was dealt a shitty hand and didn't have the will to fight it. Maybe he truly enjoys this life. Maybe the miserable old retch gene runs in the family.

The image of what I could have become flashes in my mind for a moment, a picture of me at my father's retirement party. My face would not be filled with joy and determination as his face is in the picture on his desk. No, my face would be filled with discomfort and disdain. I would have ruined the firm if my father had given me the chance. Not purposefully, but because of my lack of passion for his line of work.

Before I can start feeling sorry for Father, I tear my eyes away from the desk in search of courage. And I find it across the room. I open the liquor cabinet, no lockpicking required, and find a bottle of 25-year scotch. I pour a small glass about halfway with the amber liquid and down it in two quick gulps. It burns and I cough, but I pour another.

I carry my whiskey back to the desk and sit in my father's chair. I stare at the desk for 30 minutes before feeling tipsy and courageous enough to rummage through it.

I slide out the long center drawer. There are various rulers and scales inside, along with some sticky notes and a drafting compass.

I move to the drawer to the left. It is filled with even more basic business supplies, his old nameplate, and a stack of business cards from before he was CEO. Below that drawer is a cabinet containing binders labeled *Massachusetts Building*

Codes and another labeled *New York Building Codes.* There is a third labeled *State Licensure Documentation.* Inside are dividers labeled for each state where my father is licensed to design buildings.

I move to the right side of the desk. The top drawer contains more office equipment, graph paper, and printer paper. On this side, there is a large drawer in place of a cabinet. It has a different handle than the others; this one has a lock.

Why bother locking a drawer in an office that is already locked on the outside? That thought has me itching to get it open. I retrieve my lockpicking tools— metal skewers I found in the kitchen— from where I tossed them onto the sideboard.

I furiously wiggle the skewers around in the lock until I hear the click. It takes me longer this time, my hands shaky from nervousness and unsteady from the scotch. I pull out the drawer, and there, at the top of a pile of envelopes, receipts, and other documents, is a revolver.

I carefully place it on the desk. Why the fuck does my father have a gun in his desk? Maybe one of these envelopes has some explanation inside. I reach in to scoop up all the envelopes. When my fingers reach the bottom, I recognize that the drawer isn't as deep as it seems from the outside.

I grab the envelopes and dump them on the desk next to the pistol.

I stick my head in the drawer and examine the bottom of it. I pull on a small lip at the back center of the drawer's base and reveal a secret compartment.

The only thing inside the compartment was yet another binder. This one is unlabeled, but on the inside, there were two dividers. Behind the first divider, there is a list of names with numbers next to them:

Melanie 24265

Rachel 13923

Nadya 26043

Brit 21330

Rochelle 25704

Charlotte 27026

This continues the full length of the page.

Behind the second tab, there was another list:

Gus 10500

Robert 12000

Billy 11500

Deb 6750

This list continues for two more pages, but occasionally, there were long breaks in the lists as if they were separated on purpose.

I don't know what to make of this. Names. Numbers. Groupings. What does this fucking mean? I set the binder aside to think on some more later.

I begin flipping through the envelopes. Most have a return address from a local contractor, banks, or, occasionally, a newspaper or magazine. But then I see the familiar blue insignia of Buchanan Academy. I remove the single-page letter from the envelope.

Dear Mr. Whims,

We regret to inform you that Nathan's entrance exam scores were too low to be admitted to our program. However, with your generous donation to the Buchanan Foundation, your family has done more than enough to earn a spot on our roster. Nathan can expect an official acceptance letter in the coming week.

Respectfully,

Dean Timothy Carrigan

A pit opens up in my stomach. I slam my fist on the desk hard enough to rattle the pens.

I wasn't even supposed to make it into that damn school. My father *bought* my way in. I feel my eyebrows scrunch as I begin pacing and rubbing my temples. How many people knew? Did the teachers know? Had any of them let it slip to a student? Did Rylee know? My pulse is raging in my neck.

I take a long, deep breath and then take a long sip from my glass.

It doesn't fucking matter.

Reluctantly, I begin flipping through the envelopes again. Another envelope that is different from the others grabs my attention. The outside of this one just says *Nathan* in pink ink.

I pull out the letter, and a Polaroid slides out, landing face down. On the back, in that same pink ink, it says:

I hope this keeps you occupied on your business trip.

-S.

I flip the photo over and see Stacy, my father's assistant, naked and lying with her legs spread open on the desk I am currently leaning against. In my home. In my *mother's* home.

I drop the photo and take a step back, away from the desk. My mind goes numb and empty.

I reach for the gun. I pop open the cylinder, something I have only ever done in video games, and see that each chamber is loaded.

I pull back the hammer, place the barrel to the soft spot under my chin, and squeeze the trigger.

10

Spawnpoint Lounge

Click.

I sigh, "Well, fuck me, I suppose."

I put the revolver back on the desk and unfold the letter from my father's apparent mistress. It's handwritten in the same bubblegum pink ink as the envelope and Polaroid.

Dear Nathan,

I am so proud of you for securing the project in NYC. I'm sorry I can't make it to "assist" you on your trip to the city. I hope the picture and the gift make up for it.

It's signed with a heart and her name. Stacy.

P.S. There is a certificate of authenticity behind this letter. XOXO.

"Assist." As if fucking my father is part of her job description. I feel my face heat as I shift to the next sheet of paper. It is light blue with a gold foil seal on the left side, and next to that, it reads:

Genuine Replica: Sheriff Wilson's Peacemaker as seen in the film, Gravestone (non-functional).

A replica. Of course.

I let everything drop onto the desk's surface and return to the liquor cabinet; my legs feel wobbly and weak. I pour another glass and slowly walk back to the desk. I throw the coaster across the room and place the rocks glass directly on the shiny, wooden surface. My dad would have a conniption if he saw. "Have respect for other people's things." He would say. "That desk is older than I am. What would your grandfather say?"

"Fuck your desk, you lying piece of shit." I lift my leg and ram my foot into the side panel as hard as I can.

I do it again.

Again.

Again.

Ignoring the ache returning to my ankle, I continue kicking until I tear away the varnish, and a large gouge appears in the wood. I take a hefty swig of my drink, then pick up the lamp and hurl it at the crystal pitcher, shattering them both. Glass sprays over the sideboard and carpet.

I snatch the pens from their holder and scratch a deep line into his pristine desk pad with every single one.

I explode into rage, yelling at my father's desk, "Fuck you. Fuck you! I was never good enough!" I begin slamming my fists on the surface of the desk. "And Mom isn't good enough? Fuck you! Fuck you, you cheating, egotistical asshole! Fuck you, you lying, selfish piece of shit! I hate you. I hate you! I hate you!" I scream from the depths of my soul. No words, just a sound of unadulterated malice.

I've always held disdain for my father, but this is pure, destructive fury. I lay the letter from Stacy and the letter of authenticity on the desk and pour the rest of my scotch over them. I throw the glass onto the desk and let it shatter across its surface.

I tear to the staff bathroom and rip open the cabinet doors, remove a bottle of oxycodone, and replace it with the picture of Stacey. I storm back to Father's office and position the bottle of pills with my mother's name on it right in the middle of the letter, among the shattered crystal.

I still feel the white hot rage. More. I need to do more. I grasp the top of the filing cabinet and attempt to knock it over, but it is too heavy. Instead, I pull out the drawers one at a time and rip out the folders. I open them, letting the contents fall to the floor. Papers float down and scatter like fall leaves on the floor.

I begin to charge out of the office when my eye catches on that unlabeled binder. I get an uneasy feeling thinking about how it was hidden and how there is no explanation of who these names belong to or what the numbers represent.

Somehow, in my rage and drunkenness, I manage to take a picture of each of the pages and place the binder back carefully where I found it. My father obviously doesn't want anyone finding it. I'll let him believe it hasn't been found.

I take in the mess I made. He deserves a lot worse. I spit on the carpet and knock over a potted plant for good measure. I stumble into the hallway, locking the office door behind me.

* * *

My room is dark, just the way I left it. This isn't the ominous, threatening dark of my father's office. It is a warm, comforting darkness. The kind of darkness that hides you and protects you from the things that would grab you out in the light.

I sit in my desk chair and put a blanket over my head in an attempt to calm my thudding heart, catch my breath, and settle my mind. I can't be settled when I feel like I am careening. I whirl in my chair to face the left corner of my desk, then the right. The left. The right. The left. The right. I rock myself like a damn baby, but the repetitive motion does nothing to calm my twisting gut.

I'm torn between the feelings of guilt for wrecking my father's office and satisfaction from justice served. My father is going to lose his mind when he gets home. He is going to be absolutely livid.

I could go back to the office. I picked the lock before; I can do it again. I can fix everything. I can clean up, and—

No matter how much I tried to tidy up, I wouldn't be able to remove the whiskey stain on the letter or the damage I caused by kicking his desk over and over again, or explain the broken lamp, pitcher, and glasses.

I feel my breath go thin. I can't hide this. He deserves it. Fuck. What am I going to do? Rex. Rex would know.

I grab my headphones and call him. It takes an eternity for him to answer. Then finally—

"Rex!" I begin sobbing.

"Rex, I just wrecked my father's office. He is having an affair, and I already hated him so much. I didn't know what to do. I lost it. I—"

"Whoa whoa whoa. Slow down, Nate. Take a few deep breaths and then tell me what happened."

His voice is softer than I have ever heard, but firm. It grounds me slightly. I do as he says. I follow his instructions and breathe in for a count of four, hold my breath for a count of seven, then exhale for a count of eight. I do that four more times before Rex speaks again.

"How do you feel now?"

I take notice of my body. My breathing has steadied, and my heartbeat has slowed. I feel less shaky, but my ankle—the

119

same ankle I fucked up trying to kick open the damn shed—is throbbing. I cross my leg over my knee and examine it.

"I feel calmer, but my ankle is swollen from what I did to my father's desk."

"Tell me slowly what happened. Start at the beginning."

I tell him everything. What I found, what I did, and even what I *tried* to do. The only thing I kept to myself was the binder. I need to learn more about that on my own before I even think about sharing it with someone.

He was quiet for a moment. I begin to feel like a madman. I was about to switch into defensive mode and make up excuses for all I did when he finally spoke.

"Nate, I don't blame you for what you did to your dad's office. Trust me, I understand what it is like to have a shitty father." He pauses a moment, then, in a gentle tone, says, "You tried to kill yourself today." I hear what sounds like a sniff on the other end of the call.

"Well, I mean, I guess that's what happened. I'm pretty drunk and was even drunker then."

Another sniff. "It doesn't matter that you were drinking. You tried to kill yourself! I know your life is hard right now, but things will get better."

"I'm so fucking done hearing '*it will get better*'. What if I don't want to get better? What if it *can't* get better? This is nothing new to me, Rex. I have been feeling this way since I was thirteen years old. I am so unbelievably tired. Do you know how draining it is to want to be dead for six years? It didn't start with Rylee, but she is the final straw. I want to be gone. I want to be nothing."

I hear a gasp, then a deafening silence on the other side of the call. My heartbeat quickens again, and I feel my chest getting hot, but I don't know what else to say, so I stay hushed.

"If you can't get better on your own, then I will help you. Tomorrow, we are meeting at the cafe in Spawnpoint Lounge," he says as if it's an order.

"But you don't meet your online friends." I lower my voice and scoff, "Even if they live in the same city as you."

"I think the time has come if one of my closest friends is trying to kill himself."

"Fine. I'll be there."

* * *

I wake up with a splitting headache. I reach for the phone: 9:21 a.m..

"Fuck!" I jump out of bed, ignoring my spinning head.

Rex and I played *R.O.B.* until I passed out last night, but before we got off, we agreed to meet at 10:00 a.m.. If I get dressed quickly and run to the bus stop, I should arrive in time for the 9:30 bus. I'm cutting it close, but I should make it in time. I throw on the first clean pair of pants and t-shirt I find.

I grab some ibuprofen from the bathroom cabinet and look myself over in the mirror. I definitely look like a man who got obscenely drunk and tried to kill himself the day before.

I get my body wash from the shower and use it to clean my face. I brush my teeth, then put on a little extra deodorant and body spray. I comb out my hair and wet it down, so I don't look like a frizzy mess.

I glance over myself again. I look...acceptable.

I throw on my shoes and run out the door.

The bus is pulling into the stop as soon as I reach it. I let out a sigh, relieved to make it in time. I trudge up the steps and collapse, tired from my sprint down the sidewalk.

Now that I am on the bus, I have a moment to relax. I was so worried about making it out the door on time that I didn't have time to prepare myself for my day.

I'm about to meet Rex. In person. Finally.

We have been friends for three years. I have not spent time with him away from our computers even once. Every so often, I try to picture how he might look, but no clear picture comes to mind. For all I know, he is an elderly pervert who has been lying about his entire life. Not that Rex has told me much about his life anyway.

I know he is nineteen. I know he dropped out of school and got his GED. I know his best friend is a girl named Sierra, but they aren't dating. I know he—

"Cookie Man!"

I look up, startled, and see the man I met the other day after leaving the grocery store. "You remember me."

"Of course. How could I forget the man who supplied the cookies?"

"Well, you seemed stoned as hell, so..." I trail off.

"Don't underestimate my capabilities, Cookie Man." He stretches out his hand. "My name is Drew."

"Nate," I say as I reach for his hand and shake it. "I take it you live in those apartments." I tip my head toward the apartments behind the stop we were now pulling away from. It was the same stop he got off at the day I first met him.

He takes a seat across the aisle from me. "Nah, I live in a nice little house behind them. Those apartments are great for business, though."

"Are you a salesman or something?"

He gives me a wry smile and chuckles, "Something like that. Where are you headed, Cookie Man?"

"Nate."

"You are Cookie Man forever, my friend." He smiles again.

This guy is always so happy. It's almost annoying. "I am going to Spawnpoint to meet a friend."

"No shit? Me too. Spawnpoint is also great for business."

I nod as if I understand exactly what business he is talking about.

He pulls out a pen and a pocket-sized notebook and flips through the pages. I notice there are only names and numbers on them. "What's that?" I ask, feeling like I am snooping. It's really none of my business.

"Ah! This little notebook here is for my operation. Clients and orders, you know."

"Right. Makes sense." That makes no sense. "Theoretically, why do you think someone would have a notebook or, I don't know, a whole binder with just names and numbers in it?"

"I would assume that whoever owns that binder is conducting business that isn't exactly..." He pauses as if sorting through phrases in his mind. "...meant for public knowledge." He winks at me.

"Oh. OH!" I think I get it now. Not what my dad is doing, but Drew's profession.

He bursts into laughter. "Oh, Cookie Man, you are so innocent. I love it."

I begin to growl out a retort, but the bus squeals to a stop outside Spawnpoint. I opt for a simple hand gesture to convey my feelings. Drew only chuckles as we both exit the bus.

The exterior of the building is unassuming. It resembles all the other businesses on this street. The aspect that sets it apart from the rest is the sign. Where the other signs are chic and predictable, Spawnpoint's sign is in an old school game font, the kind of font you expect to say "Game Over" in all capital letters.

Drew and I go through the double doors together, but this is where we split. "I gotta hit the bathroom and then get to conducting my business, Cookie Man. If destiny sees fit, our paths will cross again," he says, walking in reverse toward the bathroom.

I nod at him, "See you around."

Like most of the lounge, the lobby is dimly lit with walls similar to those of a dark castle. Lanterns with LED bulbs that look like flames line the walls. A chandelier with similar lights is hanging in the center of the high ceiling. On the wall across from the front doors is a menu with prices for game room, virtual reality, and computer station rentals. A map of the building drawn in the style of a map you would find in a fantasy novel is positioned just below the menu. In front of the sign is a desk where two employees are standing by, ready to greet people, give directions, sell Spawnpoint Lounge merchandise, or take payment for use of the facilities. One of the greeters is dressed in a t-shirt; the other is in full cosplay. It seems like the employee dress code here is pretty relaxed. As long as it is related to nerd culture in some way and isn't totally indecent, it flies.

The lobby has a special requests board where customers can pin business cards, advertisements, or event fliers. Most of the time, it is filled with pages advertising used games for sale, but occasionally, you will see a request from someone looking for a tabletop RPG campaign to join or someone looking for a roommate. The board is flanked by three restrooms. One is labeled PC (Women's), one is labeled Console (Men's), and the third has a sign with a hovering wheelchair.

I make my way past the smiling greeters and into the large hall made of the same brick as the lobby, with similar lanterns every few feet. Multiple passages jut off from the main tunnel, and there is a bright light at the end. The bright light belongs to one of the few brightly lit rooms in the whole building—the library. In the library, you can find not only books, but also board games that can be checked out to be played at home or in one of the many free, first-come, first-served gaming rooms attached to the library.

Before the library is the computer room, once again with brick castle walls and dim lighting, where stations are set up to rent so you can play games or work. Rex has mentioned renting the spaces to work occasionally. He says the space makes him feel more creative.

Across from the computer room is the tabletop gaming room. This space is filled with tables bedecked with built-in dice trays and cup holders. There are also private themed rooms that can be rented for role-playing games or parties. There is one science fiction-themed, one apocalypse-themed, and two fantasy-themed rooms. This is another space I don't typically visit, but I would love to rent one of the fantasy rooms if I only had the friends to do so.

Next to the computer room is the virtual reality room. It consists of eight stations, each with a virtual reality headset, a concave treadmill, and full-body tracking sensors. A couch and projector screen are situated to the side of each treadmill, so friends can take turns and see what the player sees in the game. This room is styled to look like it was plucked directly from a dystopian science fiction movie. To keep the illusion of the dungeon passage, there is a wooden door modified to look like it is made of chrome on the inside of the room, but like a passage in a medieval castle from the hall.

The first two doors, positioned on opposite sides of the hallway, belong to The Tavern, a fantasy-themed restaurant, and the anime-themed cafe. The Tavern and coffee shop are the only two areas with a stricter dress code for the employees. In The Tavern, the waiters and waitresses wear garb exactly like you would expect to see worn in a tavern from a game, and the inside matches that aesthetic perfectly. A mixture of round and long rectangular wooden tables is strewn across the space. There is a bar with a line of large wooden kegs along the wall. A burly bartender is always behind the counter, ready to tell you tales of monsters in the nearby woods or adventurers from a neighboring village who went missing seeking to defeat the horrible beasts.

I stop in front of the door to the coffee shop. "Cafe" is written on the sign in English and again in Japanese.

As I reach for the door handle, I pause. I want to turn around. When I meet Rex, our entire relationship will change. What if he starts hating me now? What if he finds me insufferable after spending time with me in person? He only feels obligated to meet me because he doesn't want my death on his conscience.

I tug on my shirt, take a deep breath, and open the door. The room is brighter lit than the others and, for the most part, looks like a regular coffee shop. It is filled with fairly neutral colors, but with splashes of pastel color. Music from anime is playing softly over the speakers, and all the employees are wearing Japanese-inspired fashions or cosplaying characters from anime or manga. At the far end of the shop is a door leading straight to the road on the side of the building, adjacent to the main entrance.

Despite initially running behind, I arrive a bit early.

I order a brown sugar boba tea and a matcha pudding, then take a seat at a table far enough away from the counter and other customers to have privacy, but close enough that Rex should be able to find me easily.

He said he will be wearing a *R.O.B.* shirt and white sneakers. I don't see anyone who fits that vague description, so I sip my tea and people-watch to pass the time. Some of them are alone and on their phones or laptops; others are in couples or groups, talking happily and laughing a bit too loudly for my current state. I take a bite of my matcha pudding and feel some relief from the hangover still wreaking havoc on my head.

The door at the other side of the room swings open, and a woman in a baseball hat walks in. She is gorgeous. Even more beautiful than Rylee, if I am being honest. She orders something at the counter, and while her back is to me, I can't help but rove my eyes up and down her body. She is wearing a cropped t-shirt and high-waisted pants that show off her wide hips and slender waist. They hug her thighs and flare out a bit under the knee before draping over white sneakers. I begin to feel guilty and a bit creepy, so I look away.

That's when I see Drew happily bounding through the cafe right up to that beautiful girl. She had slipped on the oversized hoodie she had been holding in front of her when she walked in. She gave him a huge smile and a hug.

"Nice to see you, girl!" He says and slips something into her hoodie pocket.

She pulls away and says, "Thanks! Nice to see you too! I'm meeting someone, so I can't hang, but I'll see you again soon."

"You know I'm too busy to hang anyway, girl. See ya!" He

walks by me as he leaves and winks.

That beautiful girl smiles at me and waves. I turn to look around me. She must be looking at someone behind me. No one is there. Maybe to my left or right? I glance around. Again, no one.

By the time I turn back to the front, she is pulling out the chair across from me with a guilty smile on her face.

I look down, and that's when I see it—a *Realm of Battlecraft* t-shirt.

"Sorry, I am a bit late."

11

Q-Rex

I feel my face heating. "Rex?" I ask.

She wraps the two sides of her unzipped hoodie around her. "Quinn," she says as she reaches out her hand. I reach my hand out to meet hers, and she shakes it. Her skin is buttery soft, but her grip is firm.

"Where the fuck is Rex?" That asshole. He finally agreed to meet with me and sent someone in his place.

"Think about the name. Q-Rex. Q-Rex. Q—"

I heat even more as the truth sinks into me. "The Q stands for Quinn."

She just smiles at me.

"This entire time. It has been you." I raise my voice a bit. "The entire time?"

"Shh, quiet down, Nate." She glances around the room. "I'm sorry. I have my reasons. Would you have continued playing with me had you known? Would you have treated me the same?"

I pause a moment to consider. As if knowing I need a moment to sort through my thoughts, she sits back with her coffee and takes a sip. Her unzipped hoodie falls open, revealing her form. I gaze over her once more. She is stunning. Curly, reddish brown shoulder-length hair is poking out from under her hat. She has light hazel eyes and smooth skin that is just slightly lighter than the whiskey I was drinking last night. And her tits—I don't look at them too long since I know she is watching me, but Jesus Christ.

"Stop looking at me like that." She says and rolls her eyes. "That's why I didn't want to meet you in person. You liked me as Rex."

"I'm sorry. I am just surprised. I didn't expect this." I begin analyzing every embarrassing thing I've ever shared with her, thinking she was actually Rex and not *Quinn*.

"Does this really change anything about our relationship?" She asks.

"I haven't decided yet. It's all very weird. I have told you some very *guy* stuff."

"And you can still tell me that kind of stuff. Only now, I can respond to you in my own voice instead of using the voice changer." She gives me a reassuring look.

"But you're..." I stretch out my arm and gesture up and down her person. "...you know."

"I am well aware." She wraps her hoodie back around her and leans forward. "I get stopped at least once a day. I get shouted at in the streets. Do you understand it isn't something I can control? It is actually pretty damn annoying. It has fucked up my life more than you might realize."

"Oh, poor Quinn." I mock her girlish tone, "*I'm too hot to be a woman on the internet. I have to pretend I'm a man because I don't want extra attention.*"

She gives me an amused smile. "There's the Great Nate I've

wanted to meet for years."

I blush. "You've been wanting to meet me?"

"Of course! You are one of my best friends. I was worried you would drop me if I told you the truth. It has just gone on for so long, I felt like I was past the point of no return," she admits.

"How did you even know what I look like?" I ask, the shock of Rex's true identity finally dying down.

"I saw you a couple of times when you were a guest on Rylee's channel." She shrugged.

"And you remembered? It's been months."

"Well, I knew you were Nate, my good friend, so I committed your face to memory." She shrugged and picked at her fingernails. "I also thought you were kind of cute."

I could feel my cheeks flush at her words. She thinks I'm cute. Oh my god. She thinks I'm cute. I want to let out a whoop and break into a happy dance. But then the reason why we are meeting in the first place comes back to me.

"You're just trying to make me feel better about myself because I want to kill myself."

Her face gets serious. "No, I am telling the truth. But if you want to jump right to the nitty-gritty, let's go for it."

"Okay. I don't know where to start." I admit.

"You don't have to start anywhere. Here is what I propose. We meet up three times a week. If I remember correctly, Tuesdays, Thursdays, and Saturdays should work for you. I usually don't work until the afternoon anyway."

"You want to spend more time with my miserable ass?" I scoff.

"I want my friend not to feel alone. Knowing you could have died yesterday," her eyes begin to glisten. "I was instantly filled with regret for not telling you who I really am."

131

"So you feel guilty."

She looks at me pensively. "In part, I suppose that is true. I would spend the rest of my life thinking about what I could have done to help you. I've lost a lot of people in my life. Some I lost through death, some in other ways. I will not lose you, too. You are a good person. You deserve happiness. I'm here to help you."

She means it. She seems genuine. "Okay. We will meet here to hang out three times a week."

"I also think you should consider moving out of your parents' house and finding a therapist or maybe a psychiatrist."

"I can't leave my parents' house," I say plainly.

"Why?"

"Because then I can't afford a therapist."

"Get a job. Then find a therapist," she says bluntly.

"I don't have any skills; I can't get into a college my father would approve of, and I don't know what I would want to study in school anyway. I doubt I could afford to live in Boston, clearing tables at a restaurant." I slump back in my seat.

"Well, let's do this one step at a time. Find a therapist. I'm sure they can help you figure out what you want out of your life. In the meantime, look for a way to be happy at your parents' house and spend time with me. I'm pretty good company, right?" She laughs, gesturing to her body.

I stare at her blankly, then roll my eyes. "I will look for a therapist."

We spend the next hour talking about *R.O.B.* and TV shows. I tell her more about my parents, Marty, and Grace.

"She really made you cook?" She chuckles and takes another sip of her lavender oat milk latte.

"I actually enjoyed it."

"I could never picture you in a kitchen," she says, shaking her head.

"Well, picture it, 'cause I'll cook *you* something delicious one day," I smirk at her.

She smacks my arm. "A man who can cook? Oh, stop, you'll make me swoon." We both blush and chuckle at that comment.

"Well, I have to get to work." She picks up her cup and a purse I hadn't even noticed she had. "I'll see you at the same time on Tuesday."

I stand from my seat. "I'll see you then. Want to run some dungeons later tonight?"

"I thought you'd never ask." She smiles and walks out the door.

I remain standing for a moment, then slump back into the chair. "Holy shit." I lean back and put my hands over my face, cooling the heat that had built there over the last two hours.

I order another tea, sit down in a plush lounge chair in the corner, and analyze everything I have ever said to Quinn.

* * *

1:00 p.m. hits, and as usual, Rex comes online. Rex. Quinn. I don't know what to call hi— her anymore.

Beep-boop-whoop. Beep-boop-whoop.

"Hey, Qui-ex." Fuck.

"Qui-ex?" She laughs in an undeniably female voice.

"Sorry. I'll be honest, I don't know what I should call you anymore. You've always been Rex to me."

"Call me either. Most gaming friends call me Rex. Some call me Q."

"Hearing your real voice will take some getting used to."

"Well, get used to it, buddy. We aren't going back to the way it was."

No, there is no going back to the way it was. Rex is Quinn, and I am going to live.

Maybe.

* * *

The following week passes more easily than the previous ones.

I meet with Quinn at the arranged times, work with Marty on Wednesday, and on Friday, Grace brought the ingredients for another meal: spaghetti and meatballs. Her meatball recipe was delicious. It was worth the discomfort of mixing raw beef and sausage with my bare hands. It was cold and unpleasant to make, but the flavor of the meat with fresh herbs and Parmesan cheese was mouthwateringly good.

Despite my promise to Quinn, I still get a little drunk every day. I found my sweet spot: three drinks and a large glass of water. The buzz is perfect, and there is little to no hangover the next day. I have been working through the liquor cabinet so as not to raise suspicion from my parents when they return from their trip. After all, a little missing from each bottle is easier to hide than a lot missing from one or two. I've learned that cola with vodka is my favorite. You can't even taste the booze.

Today is the second Wednesday after meeting Quinn for the first time. Even though I had a little too much to drink last night, I rose early to meet Marty at the back gate.

"I'm going to get spoiled and lazy if you keep helping me like this," Marty says with a grin.

"Don't count on me stopping. Not until I move out, at least." I grin and pat him on his shoulder.

He looks up at me and examines my face for a moment. "You seem a bit different today," he says honestly. "Did something happen?"

"I've been spending more time with a friend. I think the time out of the house has done me good. I've been eating a bit better since Grace started teaching me to cook. That probably helps too." It's true. I do look better. My skin looks clearer and brighter, most likely from eating less garbage and getting sun on my walks to the bus stop, along with days like this, working outside with Marty.

"I'd have to agree. You looked like you hadn't slept for a week the last time I saw you."

The last time I saw Marty, I had been puking just three hours before. That was the time I grew some balls and tried straight tequila, which I now refer to as *paint thinner.*

"I think things might be changing for me. Since the summer began, I have felt like my future is just a big question mark."

I pause, hefting more lawn equipment from the back of Marty's truck.

"A couple of weeks ago, you asked me what I planned to do with my future. And I will be honest, I didn't have a damn clue. As a matter of fact, that question scared the shit out of me." I look at Marty with a frank expression. An expression I think I picked up from him. "I'm still not sure, but I think the answer is coming to me."

It's true. For the first time since I started high school and my father started grilling me about my future, I feel something like hope. This afternoon, I start therapy. Real therapy. This is not like the school therapy sessions where the counselor is paid to make us feel good about ourselves, but a real, decent therapist. Well, their reviews online are good enough, anyway.

"I'm glad to hear that, Nate. I was actually a bit worried for you." Marty shut the gate to his trailer, and I put my earbuds in. I give him a nod and get to work.

* * *

Dr. Reggie's office was in the middle of the city. I despise going to the heart of the city. It's filled with business types that make me uncomfortable. My father's office and multiple buildings he either designed or one of his designers drafted are built here as well. It is hard to look anywhere here and not feel entirely out of place.

I make my way to the third floor, which looks to be filled with different mental health offices. I speak with the man at the desk, who can't be but a year or two older than I am.

"Hello," I say a bit quieter than I need to, "I am here to see Dr. Reggie."

"Oh, Nate! Welcome to our office! You are a new patient, so I have a bit of paperwork for you to complete." He begins flipping through a veritable book of tests and authorizations, "They are all pretty standard. We have a demographic questionnaire, insurance information page, patient rights and responsibilities form, records release, BAI, BDI, and TSQ."

"BADNTSQ?" I ask, extremely confused by all the acronyms.

He lightly chuckles at my question. "They are screeners for common mental health issues we deal with here. Depression, anxiety, and PTSD."

"Right," I say as I grab a pen from him and take a seat.

"Let me know if you have any questions. Some of them are worded kind of funky," he says with an absurdly large smile.

Great. I already hate this. I complete my paperwork, cursing

Quinn over and over again with every uncomfortable question.

By the time I finish filling out the packet of paperwork, Dr. Reggie walks out. He is tall and thin with a smile very similar to the guy at the desk, but his is somehow more reassuring.

"Nate," He says in a friendly tone, "it is very nice to meet you. Come on back to my office and get comfortable. Would you like any water or coffee?"

"Um, either is fine," I lie. I have no interest in bitter bean water.

We pass a young woman with dark brown hair and black scrubs. The doctor asks her, "Would you mind getting our new patient a refreshment?"

She nods and flashes me a smile not as convincing as the doctor's, but definitely much more believable than the front desk attendant, and hurries behind a door that says kitchen.

I take my seat in his office. It is colorful and welcoming with lots of natural light. The couch is comfortable. It's not so plush that I sink into it, but it's not too firm either.

The doctor puts out his hand, and I shake it. He shakes back firmly and puts out his other hand. "Your paperwork, please."

My face begins to warm, feeling embarrassed, and then a bit annoyed. If he wanted my paperwork, he should have said so in the first place. Maybe he was offering a handshake, too. Before I could overanalyze the interaction, the girl we saw in the hall enters the room carrying two foam cups and a handful of packets.

"I wasn't sure how you liked your coffee, so I brought a few options." She placed a cup of ice water, coffee, two packets of sugar, two packets of sugar substitute, and a little cup of half and half on the side table next to where I was sitting.

"Thank you," I said, trying to catch her name on her name

tag, but it was mostly blocked by her hair, and all I saw was
—*na* and the symbol for the clinic.

She just nodded and left the room.

I turned to Dr. Reggie. He was in his comfortable-looking armchair, elbows on his knees, examining my answers on the questionnaires.

"So, Nate. What do you hope to get out of therapy?"

I stay silent for a moment, considering. "I want to figure out what I want."

"What you want?"

"Yes, sir. Everyone else seems to have their life together, but I don't know what I want."

"The idea that a young person has to have their life figured out at 18 years old is absurd. What you are feeling is valid, but it's that idea and society that have skewed your thinking. Actually, it has skewed the thoughts of the majority of young people I work with."

"Dr. Reggie," I begin to say, but he interrupts.

"You can just call me Reg."

"Okay," I clear my throat, "Dr. Reg, my entire life, I have been told that when I turn 18, I am an adult and have to go out in the real world, make money, and make my family proud."

"Anyone with guardians who give a damn about themselves or their children has said the same thing. Or something similar," he waves his hand in dismissal. "The only person you need to make proud is yourself. If you are proud and happy, but your family doesn't feel the same, disregard their thoughts because that is not your problem. That is *their* problem. It is not your job to make your parents happy. Everyone is responsible for their *own* life satisfaction and mental health, but I am talking too much." He lifts two of the questionnaires

I completed. "You scored in the *high-risk* category on both the depression and anxiety inventories. Does this come as a shock to you?"

"No."

"So you have been feeling depressed and anxious, and you seem to have issues with your family." He pauses for a long moment, placing his hands together at the fingertips and holding them against the tip of his nose. "This is how I think we should conduct these sessions; you tell me your story. Start with when you first noticed these symptoms and continue until you get to the present moment. Tell me the highlights, anything that you feel has had a major impact on your mental health. If it feels necessary, we can delve deeper into any events that have had a particularly strong impact. Therapy will change and grow as you do, so if you feel our approach isn't helping, we can adjust at any time. Does that sound good to you?"

"That sounds good." It truly does. But— "I don't know where to start."

"Is there a memory that pops into your head and makes you feel something? If there are multiple memories, choose the one that happened first. That will be your starting point."

I nodded and slowly began. "When I was around eleven years old, I found my mother passed out in the parlor..." I continue until our time is up. The doctor doesn't talk for most of the session, but listens intently and assures me that my feelings are normal and valid. He leaves me with the simple assignment to reframe my thoughts. When I think about my father and his opinions on my choices, I need to remind myself that they are *my* choices and his reactions to them are his own problem.

I feel stripped and raw. I feel refreshed and free. I feel guilty, and somehow, it feels like some past guilt has eased. Is this what it feels like to begin to heal?

On the way out the door, I booked another appointment for the same time next week.

12

An Old/New Friend

"So how was your appointment with Reg?" Quinn asks from over her caramel iced latte. Quinn was the one who had recommended him in the first place. He has apparently helped her through some tough times. Times she will not talk about with me.

"I'm not sure how it went, but I am going back next week," I say, taking a large swig of my coconut boba tea.

"I know what you mean. I felt the same way in the wake of my first few sessions. After a while, things begin to get easier. Trust me, it is worth it."

"I'm trying to trust you, but—" a familiar voice cuts me off.

"Well, well, well. Look who is already moving on!"

I look toward the entrance to the cafe, and there is a familiar face with blonde, curly hair, blue eyes, and tanned skin rolling his way over to my table with a relaxed smile on his face.

"Hayden," I say flatly. What the fuck is he doing here? Shouldn't he be unpacking his bags at his dorm in California by now? And to come up to me like he wasn't aware of my impending heartbreak and didn't warn me, the fucking nerve.

"Who is your friend?" He drifts his eyes over Quinn when he asks, then turns to me again.

"I'm Quinn," she says with a slight blush.

"I'm Hayden," he replies with his sleaziest smile.

I look to Rex, "Also known as surf'n'smurf," His screen name, the name Quinn would recognize since we were once in the same guild as him in *R.O.B.*, and played together many times.

"OH! I'm Rex!" She says, excitedly.

"No, the fuck you aren't," he says in disbelief.

"What the hell, Quinn? You made me think you were a guy for years, yet you are happy to reveal who you are to him as soon as he shows up."

"I have a good feeling about this one," she says, jerking her head to him. "My gut feelings are never wrong."

I roll my eyes.

"Well, I am certainly flattered, Quinn," Hayden says, almost blushing.

"Shouldn't you be in California?" I say a bit gruffly.

"I decided to reject my acceptance to the university in California and go to school here." He says, looking a bit embarrassed.

"When did you decide that?" I ask.

"Around the time I told my dad I didn't want to follow in his footsteps. Well, not his most recent footsteps." He turns to Quinn, "My dad created a company that manufactures surfboards and skateboards. We used to live in Hawaii, and I would surf every day. I loved it. After I got into an accident, my father decided to stop producing surfboards and moved us here to begin manufacturing other things."

Quinn looked at his chair with a downhearted expression, but he just smiled at her. "Don't worry about me; I might not be able to surf anymore, but I can still wave ski. I plan to open a small surf shop that carries adaptive boards and teach others like me how to use them. I want to bring the joy of riding the waves to everyone. Maybe it will turn into more. Who knows?"

I smile at my old friend. He has always been like this. After a short mourning period, Hayden didn't let his paraplegia get him down anymore. He always found new adventures. Actually, he could make an adventure out of anything. And now that I know he is following this path, I have even more respect for him.

He looks at me now, "Are the two of you on a date? I can leave."

"No, it's not like that," I say a bit too forcefully. I continue, trying to soften my statement, "Quinn is wonderful and obviously very—" And now I have made it weird. I clear my throat, "but no."

"Oh. Alright," he replies.

There is an awkward moment of silence, as if we are both debating bringing *her* up.

Hayden finally speaks up. "I'm sorry about what happened with Rylee."

Quinn twirls her cup on the table, staring down at it, as if acting like she can't hear our conversation.

"I know you knew before it happened," I admit. "I heard you and Dominic talking in the auditorium bathroom."

Hayden's jaw dropped slightly in surprise. "If that is the case, you also know how I felt about it. I was only told by Ashe that morning, and I hated knowing before you. I wanted to tell you. It's why I didn't ask my dad to stop at your house to pick you up before the ceremony. I couldn't trust myself not to say anything to you, and it wasn't my place to do it."

I hold my hands out in front of me, as if I am about to strangle someone. "God. Fucking Ashe." I growl, "So controlling. So manipulative. Always fucking hanging onto Rylee like she is her pet or her pretty little doll to dress up," I pause and take a deep breath. Another. I let the hint of rage subside into annoyance. "Have you heard from anyone else?"

"I have heard from Rylee, if that's what you are asking. I think she is moving to New York next weekend." He says it plainly, casually.

My gut wrenches. She will be gone. I know she isn't mine anymore. She hasn't been mine for weeks now, but she was still close. I suppose the closeness made me hold onto some hope that I would get a text asking me to come with her, a long message full of apologies, and *I love you*s. But no such message has come.

Hayden continues, "I think Ashe is moving the same day."

Good riddance.

"As far as the other guys, they are already gone, and I haven't heard from them since they left. I was kicked from our *R.O.B.* guild, and they don't respond to me through text or on Discourse." He shrugs, "I guess since we aren't together in school anymore, they don't need me. They don't need a disabled friend to make them look like good people anymore."

"They are assholes," I say.

Quinn considers this a great time for her to jump back into the conversation. "What dick heads! If I were you, I would ram them down with your wheelchair and then run over them a few times."

"Quinn, come on." I check her with a disapproving look.

Hayden bursts into laughter. "I like you, Rex. You aren't

afraid to insult me, are you? You don't tiptoe."

She explains, "No, in my experience, people with disabilities don't want you to pretend they aren't disabled. It's a part of you. I see all of you. And no, I don't *tiptoe* around any subject."

Hayden examines Quinn's face with a considering stare. After a moment, he just nods at her.

"Well, I have to go. We need to play *R.O.B.* again soon. All three of us. It was nice seeing you, Nate." He begins to turn but stops halfway. "And very nice to finally meet you in person, Rex." He winks at Quinn as he finishes turning around.

I look back at Quinn, who is nibbling on her straw and blushing. "You good?"

"Yeah, I'm good," she says and giggles. "He is super cute."

"Look, I know we are friends, but you don't need to talk to me about boys like I am your best girlfriend," I say.

"Are you a bit jealous, Nate?"

"No, I meant what I said to Hayden. Nothing is going on here." I gesture between us. "It doesn't matter if I think you're hot; you have been Rex too long for you to be more than a friend. Though I haven't hated our flirting, even if you are only doing it to make me feel good about myself."

She rolls her eyes. "Maybe we should invite him here for coffee once a week. It would be good for you to hang out with an old friend from school every once in a while, and who knows? Maybe you guys will become closer."

"You mean, maybe the two of you will become closer," I say, laughing. She rolls her eyes again, but I continue, "Alright. I get it; I'll invite him next Thursday."

She wiggles happily in her seat and slurps at the ice melting in her cup.

* * *

On my way back home, I can't help but think of Rylee leaving town. Maybe I was a fool for holding onto any hope that she would beg me to forgive her or try to convince me to move to New York with her. She won't be in Boston after next week, and maybe it is panic or hysteria, but when I get back home, I decide to text her.

Hey, Rylee!

No, the exclamation point is too much. I tap backspace with a shaky finger and continue *painfully* slowly.

Hey, Rylee. I ran into Hayden today. He told me you are leaving soon. I hope everything goes well for you in New York. I'm still in love with you. I will do anything you ask if it means we could be together. I would even study acting if that's what it would take. Or I could work as a stagehand. Please don't leave without me. Please don't go.

I delete the last six sentences and press send.

It only takes a moment to get a response. I can't bear to open it. I feel heat rising from my chest to my ears and back down to my palms, where my phone sits. I stare and stare at the notification on the screen.

Is this message just more cruelty? Is she going to crumble the pieces of my heart in her hands until she has turned the entire thing to dust? It could be the exact opposite. Maybe she wants to fix things. Maybe she regrets everything, and—I can't do this to myself. I take a swig straight out of the bottle of vodka that was sitting on my desk and try not to get my hopes up as I finally open the message.

Hey, Nate! I am moving next Thursday. Could we meet up soon? I have some things I would like to talk with you about before I leave.

She wants to meet? My breathing becomes uneven, and my upper lip begins to sweat. I don't know if I can meet with her without making a damn fool of myself.

I can do it. I can keep myself together. I have to. This is my last chance. I might never see her again. The next time I see her, it will probably be in some red carpet video, and she will be on the arm of some handsome, multimillionaire actor.

I take a few deep breaths before finally responding.

Sure. How about the cafe at Spawnpoint? Maybe Saturday at 9:30?

I lie on my bed, close my eyes, and continue deep breathing while I wait for a reply.

Sounds good! See you then!

Fuck. Fuck. Fuck.

What followed next was pure, self-inflicted torture. I spent the entirety of Thursday afternoon drinking the rest of the vodka and punching zombies in the face. I didn't stop drinking until my vision started to spin and my character died of infection. I collapsed into bed and had a horrible night's sleep.

* * *

The only thing that gets me out of bed on Friday is Grace singing at the top of her lungs. Yes, singing. Not screaming but *belting* for me to come downstairs.

"Oh, Nate! Nate! It is time to cook with the weirdo in your kitchen!" She bellowed each word, drawing out every vowel. "Time to cook! We are making something delicious!"

I slowly drag myself down the stairs, rubbing my temples with my fore and middle fingers.

"I'm sorry. What was that? Did you call?" I say in the most

147

sarcastic tone I can muster in my current predicament.

She clicked her tongue and smirked at me with a hand on her hip and a dish towel over her shoulder. "Well, you look like shit," she said a bit too frankly.

"If you have nothing nice to say, I will just go back upstairs."

She wags her finger at me. "No, sir, none of that." She sniffs at me and I rear back, "You smell like shit too." She sniffs again. "Have you been drinking?"

I blanch. I should have showered and brushed my teeth. I knew Grace would be coming today. I am such an idiot. I begin to stammer out some blatantly false excuse when Grace interrupts by placing a hand on my shoulder and looking directly in my eyes. The look on her face is warm, comforting, and so genuine that I immediately feel more at ease.

"You've told me enough during our cooking lessons to know things are hard for you right now, Nate. But don't let anything else master you. Right now, it might feel like the hooch is helping, but it is only numbing you and forcing you to put off the part where you move past the pain."

I blink. Grace is a mother. She is a *real* mother. Not a woman who had children, but a mother who nurtures, loves, and *guides*. How lucky her daughters are to have her. A twinge of jealousy churns my stomach, but I push it back. I'm lucky to have her, too. I feel a stinging sensation in my eye. Gratitude and some feeling I can't place hit me full force. I look away before finally responding, "I will be okay."

I only half believe myself. Depending on what happens tomorrow with Rylee, I may very well never be okay again.

She gives me a soft smile, then claps her hands together, "Let's get started. Today, we make tonkatsu ramen."

"You know how to cook ramen?"

"You said it is your favorite, so I learned," she says, brushing it off as if it isn't a big deal. "I brought some eggs I marinated at home so that we can have some with lunch. I can also show you how to make them. They are so damn good. It might be good to have some on hand just for a snack or to dress up that instant ramen shit you love so much."

"Thank you, Grace. This is fucking sick."

"It's rad. Yo!"

"You're so hip, Grace," I say, matching the goofy expression on her face. "But could we get cooking? I am starving."

She smiles, "We start with the pork cutlets. You like it with the cutlets fried, right?"

Grace did not touch a single item of food while she gave me instructions on how to cut, bread, and fry the meat. I selected the proper knife and prepared two bowls: one with egg and the other with breadcrumbs. I heated the oil to the proper temperature and started boiling a pot of water for the noodles, but she still didn't touch a thing.

"You've become quite comfortable in the kitchen," Grace said, noting that she didn't even have to tell me to get the water boiling for the noodles. I knew it would be part of the recipe, so when it felt like the natural time to start that step, I just went with the flow.

"We are keeping this recipe easy," she says. "Making the bone broth would be time-consuming and might be fun to try on another day, but using store-bought is fine. You can still make something delicious easily by allowing yourself a shortcut here and there. Sometimes, throwing together a meal in thirty to forty-five minutes is better. Food is supposed to delight and nourish, not stress you out to the point of not enjoying the meal once it is done."

149

"Sounds fine to me. If I'm being totally honest, I would prefer not to stand over a hot stove for two hours." It's the truth. I don't share Grace's passion for cooking and baking. Don't get me wrong, I relish the feeling of accomplishment when I eat something I crafted for myself and enjoy the process to some extent. Grace has a passion for cooking that I don't think I could ever have.

Grace shrugs, "Well, we are just about done. Grab the eggs and vegetables from the fridge. Do you have ramen bowls? A regular soup bowl or a cereal bowl is fine if you don't."

"I have ramen bowls," I say as I go for the center of the three cabinets with dishes. "My mom insisted that if I were to eat cheap instant ramen, I should at least eat it in a dignified way. I still eat it from the cup."

I place two bowls on the counter and assemble the ramen correctly: noodles, broth, vegetables, tonkatsu, and finally, one egg per bowl, sliced down the middle. My instant ramen certainly never looked this good in these bowls.

As usual, Grace and I sit side by side at the kitchen island, enjoying our lunch. It was delicious. The saltiness of the broth, the crispness of the coating on the pork, and the firmness of the noodles delighted my taste buds. And I made it. *I* made it.

* * *

After Grace leaves, I find my way back to where I usually find myself this time of day: the liquor cabinet. I stare down at the bottles. Each one is missing a few ounces of liquid. My father always buys the larger bottles, so it isn't obvious that anything is missing.

The only way I would be caught is if my father took a picture of the cart or measured the amount of liquid in the bottles. I wouldn't put it past him to do something like that, but I don't believe he cares about me enough to do it.

Vodka, brandy, scotch, bourbon, vermouth, tequila, white rum, spiced rum, I have had them all. I turn my head to the side and bunch my lips slightly.

Grace's words play back through my mind. *Don't let anything else master you.* Am I letting alcohol master me? Control my feelings? Put me off my path to healing?

I reach for the scotch, but stop halfway. Maybe I don't want to feel like a dick for going against her advice, or maybe I don't want to be a hungover asshole tomorrow, but I drop my arm and go back to my room.

I don't have to use alcohol to get through the rest of the day. No matter how stressed I am about seeing Rylee tomorrow. I can be my own master. I can get through this night without getting drunk like an idiot.

When I get back to my bedroom, I curl up in my bed and let the worst of my thoughts slam into me one by one. I let my mind wander through every possible scenario, so I can prepare myself fully for whatever may happen tomorrow.

* * *

I wake up and pace. And pace. And pace. I texted Quinn twice to verify she will be at the coffee shop by ten or earlier. I bounce on my toes while I look through my closet for something clean to wear.

I find a *Shutter Research Facility* shirt and cargo pants. To make my hair look less fuzzy, I spray it with a coconut oil spray my mom got me over a year ago and comb it through. I brush my teeth, use whitening mouthwash, and swish for double the amount of time.

And I pace more. And more. And more.

I've already been up for hours; sleeping was beyond me last night. All I could think of was seeing her again. I will feel so much joy just being in her presence, basking in her light once more. But knowing I cannot scoop her in my arms as I once would after being apart for an extended time, knowing I cannot wrap my arms around her and kiss her deeply as I did last summer, fills me with deep-rooted sorrow.

I board the bus with no time to spare. I get trapped so deeply in my gloomy thoughts that I nearly miss it. On the way to Spawnpoint, none of the hopeful expectations I had the night before came to the surface. I don't expect anything good to come from this conversation. But at the end of it, my friend is waiting for me. Rex will be here, ready to sort through everything this succubus will put me through today.

I walk up to the counter, order my usual boba tea, and find a seat at my and Quinn's usual table. I stare at the clock above the door, just as the big hand hits the six, I glimpse pale skin and copper hair in the corner of my eye.

"Hello, Nate."

13

The End

I turn a bit too quickly to seem casual, but I attempt an easy smile and say, "Hello, Rylee."

She is wearing no makeup, but she doesn't need it. She looks stunning. Her lips glisten with the same lip balm she has always used. I can still remember how it tastes. Her wavy, copper hair is down, framing her beautiful face in a way that makes the deeper shades of blue in her eyes more prominent.

Breathlessly, she says, "I'm going to go order some coffee. I'll be right back."

I nod and watch her, pleased to have another moment to ready myself. I thought I was prepared, but seeing her in person, I now realize I was fooling myself. She is dressed casually in navy skintight biking shorts that show off her small, but perfect ass and an oversized t-shirt, which masks the rest of her immaculate body. She orders something at the counter. Just a hot, light roast coffee, with nothing added.

She stops to add some milk and hurries back to me. I know her well enough to understand why she placed the order she did. She is in a hurry. Normally, she would have gotten a latte, but that takes some time to prepare. She wanted to get back to me. Maybe she ordered a quick drink because she wants to get this over with and get the hell *away* from me.

"Nate. It's good to see you." She says, cupping the warm cup in her hands. Her hands were always cold, and she was always fucking complaining about it.

"You too, Rylee," I respond, but say nothing else. If someone should start the conversation, it should be her. She is the one who said she wanted to talk. She is the one who has something to say.

"I'm sorry that I was harsh. With how I did it, I mean, how I broke up with you." She seems to struggle to find her words, staring down at her cup rather than me.

I stay silent. She's sorry? The hopes of her begging for my forgiveness and confessing her love surge back, but I tamp them down.

She finally looks up at me. "I was cruel. I didn't mean anything I said to you that night. I cannot bear to leave without you knowing how truly sorry I am."

No, she has no intention of getting back together.

"Why?" It was the only thing I could think to say.

She blinks, appearing genuinely confused by my question. "What do you mean?"

I scoff.

At this moment, I notice Quinn sneak in the door and sit right by the entrance. She is wearing her usual baggy hoodie, but also a baseball hat and sunglasses. God, she is dramatic. I push back the slight amusement and embrace the confidence boost from having a good friend nearby. She has always been the best support player.

"Why should you be sorry? You wanted to be rid of me. You

said what was needed to get rid of me."

"I'm sorry because—" She takes a long breath and closes her eyes. Without opening them, she continued. "I love you, Nate."

My mouth goes dry. And for a moment, I am frozen in place. I peel my tongue from the roof of my mouth and manage to get out the words, "If you love me, why would you break up with me and leave me behind?" Why would you *abandon* me?

She finally opens her eyes again. "You are like a brother to me," she says, twisting the knife that has been sitting in my chest since she threw it at me weeks ago. "You could never be more than that. Not anymore. Our parents have been pushing us together since we were children. What else would be expected of me but to stay with you?"

She pauses, but I say nothing. She has yet to answer my question. My confusion shifts into mild rage.

"I cannot love you the way you deserve to be loved, Nate. I cannot love you that way."

"Why?" I ask again, feeling like a skipping CD.

"I love you. I care for you more than you can know, and that is why I have to let you go. It wouldn't be fair to you. I couldn't tell you before, but I have been preparing myself. I'm not ready to tell the world yet, but I am willing to tell you." She takes a deep breath and steadies a sure gaze on me. "I'm a lesbian, Nate."

I feel my eyes go wide and my heart pulsing in my neck. All hopes of getting back together vanish entirely.

She continues, "I could stay with you forever. You are kind and fun. You were my best friend. But you deserve to be loved fully. And so do I."

I try to speak, but my voice catches. How could I have been

so blind to her feelings? I claimed to love her and be her best friend, but she has been holding onto this secret; she has been holding onto her *truth* for so long.

"You are a lesbian?" I ask like a fucking idiot.

"Yes. And I have one more thing to tell you. I'm in lo—"

"Hello." A sultry voice interrupts our conversation. I look up, and Quinn is leaning on the table, hoodie gone and cleavage on full display, staring right into my eyes. "I'm sorry for interrupting, but our date was supposed to start ten minutes ago," she continues as she rakes her fingers through my hair and gives Rylee a venomous smile.

My god, she is good. It's nice having this woman on my side, but her timing is certainly not the greatest. She must have seen the despair on my face and thought I needed to be saved.

"Uh, sorry. I was just leaving." Rylee stands, grabbing her things.

I jump up and walk her to the door, feeling frantic and foolish. "I'm sorry," I say. "I should have paid more attention. I should have known. I forgive you for being so harsh. I truly hope you find what you are looking for."

"I already have," she says, smiling. "I hope you find happiness too," she says, looking back over my shoulder at Quinn, a bit of concern on her face.

We embrace in a friendly hug. I try not to let my lingering longing for her show. She smiles at me and turns to leave.

When the door opens, I notice Ashe on the other side. Rylee passes through, and as the door closes, I see a glimpse of their embrace. I see Rylee kiss Ashe on her lips as tears glide quietly from her eyes.

The door shuts, and I am frozen.

"Nate," Quinn says in her usual voice with a hand on my arm.

"Are you okay?"

"No," I say at a hardly audible volume. My heart is in pieces. I am dying.

I run out of Spawnpoint and pass my bus stop. I run. I run. I run until I find a stop with a bus already boarding, and climb on.

The bus is crowded, so I find a place to stand near the handicap exit. I grasp the pole to steady myself as the bus lurches forward, press my forehead into the cool metal, and begin to weep.

The frustration and anger I feel threaten to send my mind spiraling into that pit again. I can accept that Rylee is a lesbian. As a matter of fact, other than her begging me to come back to her, it is the best possible outcome. The breakup wasn't so much about me as the fact that no man is an option for her. Not an issue I can correct, as I am perfectly happy being a man.

But Ashe?

Is that what she was about to tell me when Quinn interrupted? Was she about to tell me she was dating Ashe?

She has been friends with Ashe for years. How long was this going on? Was she cheating on me with her? Have they been fucking all this time?

My mind races, and I wish I had never gotten on this bus. I wish I ran all the way home just so I wouldn't have to be standing still, marinating in all this rage.

I've never felt so restless. I've never felt so betrayed.

I pushed Grace's words from my mind as I ran through the front door to the house and straight for the liquor cabinet.

I am my own fucking master. If I want to drown myself in vodka, so-fucking-be it. I spin off the cap and guzzle straight from the bottle. If I want to die, so-fucking-be it.

I can't feel this way anymore. I am done. I am done. I am done. I am done.

I grasp the neck of the bottle as I tear through my closet in search of my backpack. I find it and retrieve a pen and a piece of paper. I take a seat at my desk, shove my keyboard out of the way, and begin writing:

Dear Mother and Father,

Or Marty... or Grace...

To whoever finds my fucking body...

* * *

By the time the note is complete, the bottle of vodka is nearly empty. I fold the paper in half twice and shove it in my pocket.

I stumble my way down the stairs and to the bathroom just outside the kitchen. I remove the lid from the box of pill bottles, ignore the picture of Stacey, and ponder how much of this it would take to kill me.

I suppose enough of any of these pills would do the job, so I reach for three bottles, not even bothering to look at the label. One at a time, I unscrew the child-proof caps and dump about half the contents of each bottle into my hand.

I return the bottles and the picture of Stacy to the box, put the lid on top, and place it carefully where it was previously under the sink.

I walk to the parlor and place the bottle of vodka back in its spot in the cabinet. I grab another bottle of that sickeningly sweet wine from the crate in the pantry and lounge on the chaise I have seen my mother pass out on multiple times before.

I examine the medley of pills in my palm for a moment. So easy. It is so easy to find something to kill yourself with. Why have I been fighting this so long? I am not wanted. I am not worth being faithful to. I am not worth the honesty of those I love. I am not worth being loved back. The last few years of my life have been fallacy. Why have I been avoiding this?

The people around me will be happier when I am gone. My father won't have to deal with his failure of a son anymore. My mother won't have to feel guilty for not defending me from my father. Rex will no longer have to bear the responsibility she feels for me. Marty can quickly get through his job again without me slowing him down. Grace won't have to waste her time and money teaching me how to cook anymore. It would be better for everyone if I were gone.

I put my palm to my mouth, throw back my head, and drink deeply straight from the putrid bottle.

The pills feel like a massive bulk on their way down my throat, so I continue drinking and drinking the wine until I can no longer feel them. I relax on the chaise and wait. I wait for the silence and the peace. I wait for eternity to whisk me away.

I feel light and numb. Then I feel drowsy. Then I feel nothing at all.

And all I see is black.

14

The Hospital

"Nate! Nate!"

I hear a frantic, sobbing voice.

Chaos and lights and a pain in my chest. My throat is burning. All I taste is blood and bile.

"Nate! Nate! Please wake up!" The sobbing voice continues pleading.

My eyes are blurry, but I see the chandelier in the dining room. No. The parlor. I see a woman's face. Her eyes are red and glistening. Her blonde-gray hair is disheveled. There is something wet on my face.

My vision blurs into solid blackness.

* * *

Beep. Beep. Beep.

I see bright lights. There is a pain in my chest. My throat is still burning.

Beep. Beep. Beep.

My blurry vision begins to clear as I hear a familiar voice. A mixture of accents, "Oh, thank God!"

Someone's arms are around me. "You're okay. You are going to be okay."

I hear someone clear their throat near the door.

"You're awake." Says a gruff male voice.

I moan, barely able to make a sound.

My vision is still blurry, but I manage to make out the shape of a man. A familiar shape. Tall and lean. The only person this could be is—

"I was in Greece, and I hear my son is in the hospital."

I sit up straight; my vision has hardly steadied, but I know who this is. "I—" My throat is tight and dry. I can hardly utter a word.

"You have no reason to kill yourself, Nate. I know you are upset your girlfriend broke up with you, but this is no way to get the attention you crave so desperately." My father stands there looking at me with as much love as he ever has. None. "This is reckless, and it would be quite damning for our family if this got out."

He tosses a bottle of pills onto my hospital bed. They have my mother's name on them. "I understand what you meant by this message, and I know that you saw something in my drawer that was not meant to be seen." I swallowed hard when I remembered what I did to his office. I don't think he knows I left the clue about Stacey for my mom to find. Good.

He doesn't look me in the eyes once, seemingly distracted by something in the other corner of the room. "I will stay quiet about this incident if you stay quiet about everything you have learned since your mother and I left."

"Where is Mom?" I manage to say in a voice that sounds nothing like my own.

"She is still in Greece. I didn't tell her why I had to come back home. I just told her that there was an issue at the office I couldn't wait to see to. I would have told her had you been successful."

I blink and shake my head. His usual apathy for me is sobering. I feel like I am settling back into my body after leaving it for a short time. This is just another thing I failed at. Another thing I have failed at *twice* now. This time, publicly. I wonder if he is disappointed that I failed.

He clears his throat, and I see nothing but disgust in his eyes. "We don't need this erratic behavior in our home. I'm returning to Greece. Your mother and I will be gone for two more weeks. I expect you to be out of the house before we get back. Stay out of my office, stay out of the liquor cabinet, and return the picture you stole from me. I'll deal with your mother's..." He pauses and snatches the bottle of pills off the hospital bed and examines it. "...issues when we arrive back home. Goodbye, son."

He turns to leave the room as a man in a white coat walks through the doorway.

"Sir, are you not staying with your son?" The doctor asks.

"No. He is an adult, and you already have my insurance and billing information, so this is settled." He shoves past the doctor and leaves the room.

A tall blur of stained clothes and blonde hair darts into the hall after him. Then, I hear Grace's voice shouting, "Your son almost died. Your boy is in that room because of *your* neglect. How can you walk away from him? How is that all you have to say to him?"

In a calm voice, I hear him respond, "Grace, we no longer need your services. You are fired." My father's footsteps continue getting quieter until they are gone.

I hear Grace muttering a variety of curses as she returns to the room, wiping tears from her eyes.

I sit up. "I'm sorry I made you lose your job, Grace."

She runs to me and throws her arms around me. "Fuck him. Don't worry about me. One contract is nothing. I'm just glad you are alive."

"You found me, didn't you, Grace?"

With a haunted expression on her face, she hands me the note I had written. "I did. I noticed this sticking out from your pocket while I was waiting on the ambulance."

"Why were you even there?"

"My girls and I made blueberry muffins. I was thinking about the story you told me about the muffins you had at your aunt's house and how you haven't had homemade muffins since. I thought I'd swing by with some for you." She gestured to the small table between the two chairs for visitors. "I actually brought them with me. You can have one when the doctor says it's okay."

I look in the direction she indicated. There is a plate with a few large blueberry muffins on a small table. Flanking the table are two small armchairs, and in one of those chairs, right where my father's attention kept falling, was Rex. She looks pale and is staring down at her entwined fingers.

I open my mouth to speak to her, but the doctor clears his throat and steps away from the computer he had been typing on.

"If you all don't mind," he says to Rex and Grace, "I need to speak to Nate privately."

"We'll be back," Grace says, giving my hand a reassuring squeeze and standing from where she was seated on the bed.

163

She slips out the door with Rex following her. Rex is still silent but looks pained, like she is ready to burst with words and tears.

I look up at the doctor who is now at my bedside. He shines a bright light in my eyes and holds up his finger for me to follow with my gaze. "You are very lucky, young man. Had you not drunk yourself to the point of profuse vomiting, the pills you took would have had the time to work, and you would be gone." He returns to the computer and begins scrolling through reports from my time in the hospital so far. "You expelled most of the medications yourself, which gave you the time for the ambulance to arrive. We removed the remaining toxins from your system upon your arrival. You gained and lost consciousness multiple times for approximately twelve hours." Twelve hours? Has Grace been here the entire time? Worried and waiting for me. The doctor continued, "You will need to remain in our care for the next few days. Since this was clearly an attempted suicide, you will be under psychiatric watch for at least the next 72 hours. We also need to be sure you don't suffer any neurological effects from the toxins you ingested, so you will need continued neuropsychological evaluations until the extent of the damage is determined."

I nod to him. This is a lot to take in. I never considered how it would damage my body if I survived. I didn't expect to need to worry about it.

"There will be a counselor coming to speak with you after you have had a bit more time to wake up and take in what has happened."

"Uhh, thank you, Doctor." I manage to say.

"You're welcome, Nate. Enjoy the company of your friends, but also get some rest. There will be nurses coming in and out, doing tests and checking your vitals now and then."

I nod to him as he exits the room. A moment later, Rex and Grace return.

Apparently, it is now Rex's turn to cry over me. She bursts into tears as she slams into me, hugging me tightly. "Damn. Easy, Rex. I am barely alive."

She smacks my arm and scolds me through her tears, "How can you joke like that? You could have been dead. You really could have been dead!"

"Are you seriously angry with me right now?"

Grace hums a tune and meanders to the other side of the room to give us some privacy.

She begins sobbing now. "No, I am angry with myself. You were obviously upset after meeting with Rylee. I should have gone after you. I should have dragged you back to the cafe and insisted you sit with me and talk it over. I let you go home, thinking you just needed time to yourself. I should have never left you alone."

I wipe her eyes and bring her in for a tight hug. "It is not your fault I did this. You are one of the few people who make me feel alive. Thank you for being here for me now."

We both force smiles onto our faces. I could tell her smile was much more convincing than my own, as if she had too much experience faking a smile.

I try not to think about how little I know about Rex's past and ask, "How did you know I was here?"

"Okay. Don't get mad at me. One day, when we got coffee, you left your phone at the table when you went to the bathroom. I took that opportunity to set myself up as your emergency contact. Grace saw that when she used your phone to call the ambulance and called me, thinking you would need a friend." Rex shrugged and looked to Grace, who was twiddling her

165

thumbs in the corner chair.

I glanced between them. "Thank you both."

Rex takes my hand and, with tears in her eyes, asks, "Why did you do it, Nate? Was it Rylee?"

I shook my head. "In a way, yes, but also no. I don't blame her. I felt like my life was a lie. My father doesn't care about me. My mother pretends to out of maternal obligation. But Rylee? She was everything. I was so in love with her; it was the only genuine thing in my life. That turned out to be a lie as well. Finding out she is a lesbian was freeing, like it wasn't my fault she ended things. But it was as if all the feelings she had for me were one big act, like my life was just another play she was performing in, and she did a damn good job. As soon as I saw her kiss Ashe—" I pause, trying to piece together the flood of emotions I felt in that moment. "I was scared I kept happiness from her, and I was angry she held onto me when I could have been finding my own happiness too."

* * *

Grace and Rex left the room again when the psychiatrist arrived to conduct her first evaluation. They were going to go to their homes, but the doctor asked them to sit in the waiting room if they had time to spare.

She was a short, serious-looking woman with black, chin-length hair and tan skin. Her voice was deceptively light.

"Have you attempted to end your life before?" asked Dr. Sanchez as she adjusted her turquoise glasses.

"I tried to hang myself a couple of weeks ago, and I tried to shoot myself with a prop revolver. I didn't realize it wasn't a functioning gun until nothing happened." I surprised myself by sharing so much, but something about my father's reaction resonated through me. He didn't care. I should dismiss the things he has said to me just as he dismisses me.

Maybe if I start with honesty and work my way through, I can come out on the other side of this. Maybe I can find something real on the other side.

"Did you seek medical attention after you attempted to hang yourself?"

"No."

"Have you been experiencing any shortness of breath, coughing fits, or chest pain?"

"Umm, maybe." I still feel dazed and unsure.

"I'll advise your doctor to run tests on your heart, lungs, and central nervous system. It's common to have lingering issues in these areas after an attempted hanging. I don't want to pressure you too much first thing after regaining consciousness, so I will leave and speak with your friends. Get some rest, and I will see you again in the morning."

"Wait, why talk to Rex and Grace?"

"Friends and family are important sources of information when determining if a suicidal patient is ready for release."

I ask the doctor, "You can't just take my word for it, huh?"

"That is what we are trying to determine. It is also important to understand what kind of support system you have once you are released."

"Oh." I glance down at my hands. I feel like a child. I can't be trusted to be on my own. I'm a flight risk.

I look up, but the counselor is already gone. I spend the rest of the evening watching a show I had never seen before on a grainy television and feeling the weight of the nurses' pitying stares as they pass my door.

167

* * *

My sleep is interrupted numerous times through the night by nurses checking my vitals, swapping out my I.V., or administering more medication.

My doctor had apparently ordered an MRI and a CT scan, so first thing in the morning, I am carted off to one dark room after another to make sure I didn't ruin my lungs, heart, or brain when I tried to hang myself.

I was finally allowed to have one of Grace's muffins after the tests were done. I had never tasted something so delicious in my life. I could taste the care and love in each bite. Or maybe that was just the cream cheese swirl twining between the blueberries. I will have to put these muffins on the list of dishes I want Grace to teach me.

I stop mid-chew as I remember I am no longer welcome in my father's house, and Grace is no longer employed by my family anyway. I imagine my days of cooking with her are over. I wipe a crumb from my hospital gown and continue eating slowly. I savor every moment the muffin is in my mouth and let a tear or two fall from my eyes.

"That must be one hell of a muffin. Can I have one?"

Startled, I wipe my eyes and quickly swallow what was in my mouth.

"Hayden! I definitely wasn't expecting to see you here."

"Quinn messaged me on Discourse and told me you were here. She didn't tell me what happened, though." He rolled up to the side of my bed opposite the door with two iced coffees and boba tea in a drink carrier on his lap.

"Just an unfortunate accident," I lie. He hands me the boba tea as I reluctantly part with one of Grace's muffins.

"Well, you were there for me after my accident, so I should be here for you after yours." He gives me his signature wide, easy smile and takes a sizable bite from the muffin.

I smile back at him. "I'm glad you are here."

After half an hour of small talk and avoiding discussing the real reason I was in the hospital, Hayden's gaze darts to the door, and he blushes.

"Well, hello, gentlemen!" Rex says as she strides to sit in the visitor's chair directly next to Hayden.

He stiffens slightly but takes a deep breath and hands her one of the iced coffees. "For you, m'lady."

Her eyes widen in surprise, "Oh, thank you!" She takes the coffee, "Did you know I would be here? I don't think I told you I was planning on coming this morning."

"It was just wishful thinking." He shrugged.

We all sat in silence for a moment, my two friends staring at each other. I'm glad I am here to see this. Whatever this is, whatever this is turning into. I'm glad I am here for it.

Dr. Sanchez came in at that moment, breaking our comfortable silence. "I'm sorry to interrupt your visit, Nate, but it is time for your appointment." She looked at my friends. "It should only take an hour or so. I would suggest you go get coffee and come back, but I see you have that covered already."

"No worries." Hayden faces Rex and suggests, "How about lunch at the deli down the road?"

"Sounds perfect," Rex replies quickly, then says to me, "We will be back in about an hour. Promise."

Once the door closes behind my friends, the doctor continues. "Good morning, Nate. How are you today?"

"I feel more like myself, I guess."

"I am assuming that young man is another one of your

169

friends."

I strike the doctor with a serious expression. "Yes, that is Hayden. He doesn't know why I am here, and I would prefer it to stay that way."

She lifts her hands, "Say no more. I will not ask him any questions. I think Quinn gave me most of what I needed anyway." She takes a seat in the farther of the two visitor's chairs. "Now, let's get to more of the questions I have for you."

I say nothing.

Dr. Sanchez clears her throat. "We'll just jump right in then. Are you currently seeking mental health treatment?"

"My first meeting with a therapist was last week. I plan on meeting with him each Wednesday afternoon."

"That's excellent, Nate. Your first experience with a therapist can be jarring. It can open old wounds and leave you feeling bare and emotionally raw. Do you think that is what spurred your most recent suicide attempt?" She readies her pen on her notepad, waiting to take down my response.

"No." I should say more.

"Usually," The doctor continues, "a suicide attempt is the culmination of events. A person may experience hardships and depression for an extended period of time, powering through each day with dying on the back of their mind. The attempt typically takes place after a significant triggering event has occurred. Does this sound like your experience?" She poises her pen once more, leaning forward in her seat.

I need to be brave. The only way to move forward, to get out of this hospital, is to take the first step. I take a deep breath, and the tears begin to pour out before the words. "I—I learned that my relationship with my girlfriend was a lie for *years*. I learned my ex was probably cheating on me with her best friend for

God knows how long. But that was just one of the many things that were piling up and up and up. I'm a failure and a loser. My parents abandoned me. Most of my friends abandoned me. Rylee abandoned me. I'm *nobody* and I am going to stay a *nobody*." I can barely hold back my tears, but I continue, "I am nothing to my family but a disappointment. I have no idea what to do with my life. How the hell does anyone really know what they want for the *rest of their life?*"

I hold my head in my hands, nearly shaking, but I manage to contain my tears. My breath is quick and shallow, but I force myself to take deep breaths and steady myself. Once I am sure I have mastered my emotions, I look up to see Dr. Sanchez looking at me with a soft smile.

"You are doing an excellent job, Nate. Thank you for sharing that with me. Making yourself vulnerable, especially with a stranger, is not easy." Her smile widens. "I'd like to let you in on a secret, Nate. Nobody knows what they will want for the rest of their life, at least, not at your age. You aren't born with a set destiny, and your calling doesn't just dawn on you one day in high school. It is fine not to be sure of what you want."

"All my life, my teachers, my parents, my grandparents, and even my school counselors have been telling me I have to know what I want to do before I even turn eighteen."

"That mentality forces children to choose a path they end up hating. Life isn't about finding your singular purpose. You will learn new things about yourself throughout your life, and what you want can *change*. That's the beauty of life. It is ever-changing. For now, find what brings you peace. Do what fills you with contentment, and maybe you will find joy."

A feeling of foolishness settles in me. She is right. This is my life. Mine. It isn't up to anyone else to determine how I live. It isn't up to them what I do for money or for fun. I determine my purpose.

She continues, "I'm sorry to hear about your girlfriend. It is hard when long-term relationships end. It is even harder when you learn they aren't who you thought they were. Over time, the pain from it will lessen. You will be able to trust and love again."

"I don't feel like I have ever been loved. I don't even think I know what it should feel like."

Dr. Sanchez gives me a frank, but soft expression, "Are you trying to tell me those two women I talked to, Grace and Quinn, don't love you? It didn't seem that way to me."

I don't respond, but take a moment to consider. Grace took time out of her day off to bring me muffins. She bought ingredients with her own money to teach me how to cook so that I could have decent meals. She called my best friend to tell her I am in the hospital and to find me more support. She cried for me and held me when I woke. She chased down my father, screaming at him because he treated me harshly. I suppose that is love, the love of a mother I never had.

And Rex, she reached out to me when everyone else abandoned me. She checked in with me daily, let me talk about everything that was troubling me, and insisted on meeting with me three times a week because she knew I was hurting. That was love, too, the love of a friend, the love of a sister.

I dropped my head and placed my hands over my face as quiet tears began to fall from my eyes.

Dr. Sanchez was silent a moment longer, but placed a gentle hand on my shoulder. She continued, "The doctor told me about your father's visit. If your biological family doesn't love and support you, you can choose your own family. Don't sit

172

around letting people hurt you. Surround yourself with people who lift you."

Choose my own family? Just let mine go? Let all my father's expectations go? Let my mother's remorse and reckless behavior go?

I keep my face covered and break into a full sob. I can accept it. I will accept it. Eventually.

I sniff and say, "You're right. Thank you."

"I usually am," Dr. Sanchez chuckles. "I think that is enough for now. I'll give you some time to rest and think. We will continue later this afternoon."

When she walks out the door, I am left in silence. For the first time in a long time, I don't immediately attempt to choke out the silence. I let it hit me. I let everything that I did crash into me. I let everything I had before, and everything I cherish now, cycle through my head, much like the vision I had in the brief moment I was hanging from my ceiling near unconsciousness.

I had only a moment to be with my thoughts, as Rex and Hayden returned soon after the doctor left. They were smiling and laughing. It made my heart ache with gratitude.

Hayden greets me with a high-five, then positions his chair flush with the one Rex just plopped into. She leans forward and tosses a wrapped hot sandwich next to me on the bed.

"I couldn't let him be the only one bringing you gifts. I'm sure it is better than the food they have here. You like ham, right?"

Of course, she remembered. "Nice! Thanks." I get to work on the sandwich, not realizing how hungry I was. I suppose puking your guts up, having your stomach pumped, and gaining and losing consciousness for twelve hours leaves you ravenous.

After I finish my sandwich, Hayden says, "Well, I will give

173

the two of you some privacy. I had plenty of time with Nate this morning. I can't hog him all day."

"See you later, man."

Before he leaves, he gives Rex a knightly kiss on the back of her hand and says, "I'll see you later." He winks at her as he heads across the room.

When the door clicks closed, I snap my head to Rex. "What the hell happened between you two at lunch?"

She merely shrugs.

I decide not to pry.

Rex and I spend the next three hours in relaxed silence, watching TV and discussing what I spoke to the psychologist about when she and Hayden went to get lunch.

"I feel lighter. I realize now that I can find a way to accept myself. I am still a long way from where I want to be, but I can get there." I pause, uncomfortable with this new feeling of being truly vulnerable with a friend. "I have you to thank for that. I appreciate your friendship more than I have the words to explain. Thank you, Rex, thank you."

Through blurry eyes, I see her lunge for me with open arms and a deluge of tears streaming down her cheeks. She embraces me tightly. "Thank *you*, Nate. You have no idea how much your friendship has helped me. I—" She sits down next to me and drops her hands to her lap. Her eyes are marked with trepidation, but she continues, "I was hurt by a man before, many men, actually. I was abused in more ways than one, and you—" She presses her hand across her mouth and squeezes her eyes shut as if trying to hold in her sobs. "I've been doing everything I can to get stronger, to learn to stand up for myself, to defend myself if I have to. But it was you who showed me I could feel safe again, that I could *trust* a man again. Thank

174

you."

I squeezed her hand. She has hinted at a rough past before, but this is the most she has ever told me about it. As tempted as I am to press her for more, she clearly isn't ready, so I smile at her and say, "You're welcome, Rex."

We stare at each other in a long moment of mutual appreciation until she finally sighs and smiles at me. "Well, I should go. I'll see you tomorrow."

She heads to the door. "Message if you need me." She waves and closes the door behind her.

I lay my head back on my pillow and enjoy solitude with the weight lighter on my chest.

* * *

I wake up to a light tapping sound.

I open my eyes and see Dr. Sanchez standing in the doorway, knocking gently on the open door, balancing two cups of tea in one hand. "Is now a good time?"

I nod.

She extends one of the teas to me. I immediately take a sip, desperate for something to wash away the grogginess.

"Great!" She smiles, "Do you regret surviving your suicide attempt?"

I nearly spit out my tea. "Whoa, right back into the deep end, huh?" I cough and clear my throat, but answer her, "As soon as I saw my father yesterday, I wished I had been successful. But now, no. I don't regret surviving at all. I think I have more to live for than I realized."

A large smile blooms on her face. "That is really great to hear,

Nate."

"Will I be able to leave soon? I'm beginning to feel a bit restless being stuck in this room."

"That's understandable, but we need to keep you under observation for at least one more day to ensure you are ready. What do you plan to do when you arrive home?"

I don't even have to think about it. "I'll probably play some video games on the first day. Then, I am going to look for a new place to live and pack up my things."

"Are you feeling anxious about finding a new place to live?"

I bite my tongue. I shouldn't have said that. Of course, a big change like that would raise a red flag to a psychologist evaluating a suicidal person.

"No, I'm not nervous about it at all," I lie. "I'm excited, actually. I need a fresh start. I think it will help." All of a sudden, my words start feeling more like the truth.

"That is great! If it does get stressful, I'm sure one of your friends will be happy to help. Don't be afraid to reach out to Quinn, Grace, or Hayden if it becomes too much to deal with on your own."

I nod.

"Now, according to the doctor's notes, you took a variety of drugs during your attempt. Do you still have access to these?"

"No, I think my father got rid of them all." As far as I know, this isn't true, but it's possible he went digging for my mom's stash after he saw the bottle I left for him to find. And it feels like the right answer to get me the hell out of here.

"Are there any *functioning* firearms in your home?"

I clear my throat to cover a chuckle, thinking back on the prop gun she was clearly referencing with her emphasis on the word *functioning*. "Not that I know of."

176

Dr. Sanchez looks up from where she was scribbling on her notepad. "Fantastic. Like I said, we need to keep you here for observation one more day. As long as your physician clears you, you are free to go tomorrow evening. I will stop by tomorrow to deliver your safety plan. I will also call Quinn and Grace with instructions for them. I would usually require you to speak with a therapist within 72 hours of your release; however, you already have an appointment with a therapist scheduled for next week, so I will call you to check in between your release and your next appointment. I also think you could benefit from seeing a psychiatrist. There is no shame in taking medication to manage depression and anxiety. Do you have any questions for me before I go?"

"What sort of instructions will you give to Rex and Grace?"

A look of confusion shows on her face for a moment. "Rex? You call that lovely girl Rex?"

I smile, "It's a long story."

"Very well. It is standard in these circumstances to give instructions to friends or family to remove dangerous objects from the home and to keep an eye on the patient for a while."

"Oh, okay. I guess that makes sense."

"Any other questions?"

No, but I pause as if I am thinking about it before I respond, "No."

15

A Second Chance

Just as she said she would, Dr. Sanchez returned Tuesday afternoon to deliver my safety plan, which was basically just a more detailed outline of what she had said to me the day before.

Once again, before leaving, she asked if I had any questions.

Of course, I didn't, but I couldn't look like I wasn't seriously considering it, so I looked very thoughtful for a moment before saying, "Um. No, I don't."

"Very well. If you feel the desire to harm yourself, please call this number," she hands me a pamphlet for the suicide help line and points to the web address, "Or go on this website if you would prefer to chat with someone online. It was good to meet you, Nate. I sincerely wish you well."

I nod, "Thank you. It was nice meeting you, too."

Despite being cleared by a psychologist, I wasn't released by my physician until Thursday morning. When I tried to hang myself, I developed something called acute respiratory distress syndrome. I thought the tightness in my chest was just my usual anxiety. I was coughing and running out of breath easily, but I never went to the doctor. How could I admit to them what

I tried and failed to do? I could breathe well enough, so I wasn't worried.

Because I ignored it, it turned into pulmonary fibrosis. The doctor spent Tuesday and Wednesday running more tests to determine the extent of the damage. Thankfully, it is not a severe case, but my lungs will most likely give me some trouble for the rest of my life.

I continued receiving visitors throughout my entire stay in the hospital. Quinn and Grace visited me each day. Grace brought me chocolate chip cookies and ramen one day, then lasagna and cinnamon rolls the next.

Hayden visited me once more, and to my surprise, Marty came to see me too. "I'm not good at this stuff, but Grace told me you were here, and I had to check in. Feel better, kid," he said as he handed me a card and a balloon. He didn't stay very long, but I told him my father had kicked me out during his visit. His response was to call my father an ass and offer to help me move my things as soon as I find a place to live.

Today, I'm leaving the hospital with new prescriptions, an oxygen concentrator rental, and a warning that I shouldn't exert myself until I have a follow-up with a pulmonologist.

I go through the automatic glass doors and step onto the busy sidewalk. I close my eyes and let the heat of the morning sun warm my face. The city feels new. Despite the stink of the metropolitan street, it all feels fresh.

* * *

I arrive at Spawnpoint early, so I examine the bulletin board in the lobby. I have to find a new place to live, and I suppose this is a decent place to start my search. At least know these people have somewhat similar hobbies.

A room in a two-bedroom apartment is available three blocks away. "Must be cool with sharing a room with my pet snake" is scrawled along the bottom of the flier. Uh, no, I'm not cool with that, thanks.

There is another apartment with an available room nearby. The price is fair, but there is a note that says, "the living room doubles as my ska band's practice space. We practice three days a week until 10 p.m.. Only inquire if you can jam." God spare their neighbors.

"Any luck?" Rex asks as she casually leans against the wall next to the board.

"There are a couple of options. I'm not sure how I feel about living with strangers. Hell, I don't know if anyone would even take me in, considering I don't have a job and only have enough money to make it three or four months."

She hums, "A pickle indeed. Let's go get some coffee."

I order my usual tea and an ube donut.

I blame my horrible sweet tooth on Grace. She has been flooding me with cookies and cakes since she started showing me around the kitchen.

"Is Hayden joining us today?" I ask as we make our way to the small corner table, which seems to have become *our* table.

"Nope. It's just us." She replies with a smile.

"It seems like the two of you have gotten pretty close," I say, trying not to pry too much.

She blushes, and a massive grin appears on her face. "He asked me out at that lunch date we had while you were in the hospital." She started sliding the pendant on her necklace back and forth on the chain.

I smile excitedly at her, but before I have the chance to say anything, she interjects. "Hey! I never said I agreed to go out with him!" She says, as if it isn't apparent that she did.

"But you did." I didn't actually know for sure, but I know Rex, and just looking at that blush and seeing her general nervousness...I am pretty damn sure. If she hasn't yet, she definitely plans to.

She snorts and rolls her eyes. "Yeah, okay, we went bowling last night and are going out to dinner this weekend."

"I fucking knew it! I have a good feeling about you guys."

"Thanks! Me too. He is such a nice guy, and despite everything he has been through, he stays driven and hopeful. I admire him for that."

I nod and smile at her, but try not to feel ashamed that I couldn't power through my struggles as Hayden did. I tried to take the easy way out, but I am here now. I will keep going, and someday I will be someone worth admiring, too.

"So what about you? Based on what you said at the hospital, it sounded like you were ready to let Rylee go. Do you think you will date anytime soon?"

"If I meet someone amazing and irresistible, I might ask them out, but first, I want to take some time to figure out who *I* am and what *I* want. I've always been Rylee's boyfriend, or my father's disappointment. It's time to see how great simply being Nate can be."

She gives me a broad smile, and something shimmers in her eye. "I'm looking forward to seeing what you do, and I will be here every step of the way if you will have me." She takes a sip from her coffee and sits up straight, suddenly looking very serious. "Now, I have given it some thought, and I've decided, if you want, you can live with me."

"What?" I say, nearly spitting out my tea, "If this is because you feel guilty that your efforts over the past few weeks didn't stop me from—"

She cuts me off, "No! That is totally not why. I have a two-bedroom condo. It was left to me by my grandmother. I haven't been able to bring myself to clean out her old room, but if you are willing to help, the room is yours. I won't even charge you rent for the first couple of months to give you time to find a job. The place has been paid off for years anyway."

I don't know what to say. My heart thuds. I've never had to share space with anyone before. It sounds like a sweet deal, though. Taking her offer could fuck with our friendship, but saying no just doesn't feel like an option. "Will living together make things weird between us?"

"I don't know. I guess we will find out," she says, with a grin that is daring me to refuse her.

If I say no, she will fight me on it until I change my mind. I might as well save myself the trouble.

I smirk at her. "I guess we will."

* * *

I take my time going back home. I vaguely remember lying in a pool of my vomit when I was shaken half awake on the day I— God, it is going to smell so bad.

I am in no hurry to return to the hellhole. I stroll the city sidewalk, letting the mob of pedestrians veer around me until I find a stop with a loading bus, a slower echo of my frantic run from just a few days ago. A feeling of panic mixed with shame makes me pause on the bus steps. I take a deep breath, letting the feeling pass, and continue forward.

I close my eyes and rest my head on the window for the

entirety of the bus ride. I don't know if I will feel anything once I pass the threshold to the place I once called home. I don't know if I will break down. I don't know if it will make me want to make another attempt to end my life.

I feel fragile. I feel like I can't trust myself, like *I* don't even know what I will do.

As I enter the front door, I am greeted by a bouquet of balloons and a whole chocolate cake, courtesy of Grace and, thankfully, no pile of five-day-old vomit. A feeling of guilt trickles through me. I know the vomit is gone because of Grace, too. I expected to feel something more than that, though. The last time I left this house, I was unconscious. Nearly dead. Shouldn't I feel more?

I feel grateful to be alive, but I don't feel any relief being back here. This place won't be my home in a couple of days. I don't know if it ever really was. I walk up to my room. It has become an absolute mess since the summer began. It didn't bother me before. I ignored the smell of stale liquor, the sight of crunched soda cans on the floor, and pairs and pairs of unwashed sweatpants. Now, I can't ignore it. If I make a mess like this in Rex's condo, she would go berserk.

I could sit down at my computer and play the day away, but I have been lying in a hospital bed for days. I don't feel like sitting still right now.

I return downstairs to track down a trash bag and get to work clearing my room of the garbage. Before taking the full bag downstairs, I gather all the clothing strewn over the floor into my hamper. Before tossing the bag in the outside bin, I stop by the laundry room.

I throw the clothes into the washing machine and step back to examine the various buttons, dials, and compartments. It's intimidating. I've never had to wash my own clothing before. It's only sweatpants and t-shirts. There is no way this should be so complicated.

What does it mean to wash something on a *heavy* cycle? Are sweatpants heavy, or does it mean coats and blankets? No, it can't mean blankets because there is also a setting called *bedding*. Or maybe *heavy* refers to the level of filth on whatever you are washing. I haven't been bathing enough, but it's not like there is mud and shit all over them. I shrug. *Normal* it is.

I find some detergent packs in the cabinet above the washer, toss one in, then toss in another one for good measure. I hold down the start button. The machine makes a whirring noise, and the sound of water pouring into the drum fills the room. I wiggle my shoulders back and forth in a victory dance, which I must have picked up from Grace. Jesus. I'm turning into as big a goof as her. I find myself smiling, and a soft, warm sensation fills my chest at the thought.

The feeling turns icy once I go through the back door to take out the trash. The lawn is freshly mowed, the bushes are trimmed, and the walkway is immaculately edged. Marty did this alone yesterday. It strikes me now that the last time I helped Marty with the yard work was the *very* last time. No more feeling of contentment after getting the grass along the side of the house cut perfectly straight with the trimmer. No more chats with Marty after the job was done. I found myself looking forward to those days, standing in the morning sun, sweating my ass off.

Before returning to my room, I find the multipurpose cleaner under the sink. I grab a couple of rags and the vacuum from the laundry room closet. Yet more basic housekeeping tasks I've never completed.

* * *

I understand now why my parents hired a maid. Cleaning the surfaces in my room and bathroom isn't particularly difficult, but it is annoying and time-consuming, as is vacuuming the floor. I had to unplug the damned thing when the cord had no slack left, so I had to find a new outlet twice before I was able to finish the job. Whatever. It's done.

Before I return the cleaning supplies downstairs, I take the bedding off my mattress. My clothes are done washing, so I switch them over to the dryer and stuff the washer with my sheets and comforter. At least the setting for this load is obvious. Bedding.

The only thing left to do is pack my things.

Back upstairs, I find my old luggage in the back of my closet. All the clothing I wear will fit in these two bags. I can leave the rest behind.

By the time I filled the bags, my closet looked like it could have easily belonged to someone else. The ridiculous amount of clothes my mother bought for me was all that was left, and all of a sudden, it looked like a much more reasonable amount of clothing; now that the items I actually wear were removed from the collection.

I riffle through the miscellany below the unworn clothing. There are small piles of books, mostly books I had to read for my literature classes. Shoved between the books and the wall sits my backpack, still full of old assignments. And on the other side of the books sits a crate filled with old cords and game controllers.

I reach in and remove the makeshift noose I tied only five weeks ago. I rub my chest and think about the permanent damage to my lungs. I'm a fool and a poser. Had I truly wanted to die? If I did, wouldn't I be dead? Wouldn't I have made sure?

I continue ruminating on my motives and desires as I make my way to the kitchen.

No. No. I wanted to die. I still want to die, but I have to power through. I have Marty, Grace, Rex, and now Hayden, who are looking out for me and wholeheartedly want me alive and well.

I retrieve the scissors from the drawer.

If I can't live for myself...

I make a single cut in the cord right at the top of the knot.

I will have to live for them...

I cut again at the part that dug into my neck the most, the center of the loop.

But only until I find a way to live for myself. Only until I find something to wake up for every morning.

I let the pieces of wire fall into the trash bin and stride back to my bedroom with my head high and an invisible weight off my shoulders.

* * *

My clothes, computer desk, and computer are all I need to bring with me. There is already a bed in my soon-to-be room. Rex told me that as long as I don't mind sleeping in a bed someone died in, I can use her grandmother's. I will buy a new mattress in the morning. Although it does seem morbidly fitting to sleep in a deathbed after basically coming back from death myself.

I find a box and throw my backpack in, which is now filled with a few button-down shirts, a couple of pairs of slacks, and some formal shoes. I will need to find a job, which means job interviews. I can't go to an interview in jeans and a t-shirt after all. I also pack a few of the books from the stack, an extra charging cable for my phone, and anything I usually use to get ready in the morning and for bathing.

That only leaves my computer, the desk it sits on, and my chair. I will worry about all of these in the morning since I have plans to play with Hayden and Rex tonight.

I take another look around my room and at my bed, now made with fresh sheets and blankets. It is my last night here, in this house and room. I can't bring myself to feel sad about it. There is no bittersweet feeling like I once heard friends mention when they talked about leaving home.

The only thing I feel is uncertainty. I've never worked before. I've never lived in close quarters with someone else. I've never shared a bathroom or chores with another person, let alone a girl. Living with Rex feels tricky. I played it cool at the coffee shop, but thinking of sharing such a small space with her, especially now that she is dating my friend, has my stomach twisting.

I sit in my desk chair, it is comforting, the only place in this house that feels like home. I imagine it will feel even more comfortable in a home that doesn't have my father's presence tainting it.

Beep boop whoop. Beep boop whoop.

"Hey, Rex."

"Hey, Nate! Tomorrow is the big day!"

Hearing Rex's excitement eases the tension I was feeling.

"Tomorrow is the big day," I say, and I find myself grinning.

16

Condo Sweet Condo

The place is small, like half the size of the second story of my parents' house, small.

I wave goodbye to Marty as he leaves the apartment. He helped me bring my things upstairs, but quickly had to get back to work.

"It's not much, but it is pretty cozy and free. Well, free for me anyway. It is four hundred dollars a month for you, which includes water, electricity, and internet. You don't have to pay for three months or until you find a job, whichever comes first." Rex is standing in the living room, looking humble and a little reluctant.

I nod to her, examining the room. Like she said, it *is* cozy. The living room has a plush, beige-colored couch and two armchairs. One is teal, and the other is yellow. Each seat has a soft-looking blanket and a pillow or two placed neatly on it. There is a sliding glass door that is draped with amethyst curtains that leads to a small balcony. A brown coffee table sits on a fluffy orange rug in the center of the room. Rex's computer desk sits against the wall across from the sofa. Just like the rest of the room, it is impeccably tidy with a neat line of stuffed animals that I immediately recognize as creatures from many of the games we have played together. Next to the desk is a floor-to-ceiling bookshelf overflowing with books and board games.

"Do you have a lot of game nights?" I ask. I can't help but think of Grace and her daughters.

"Yeah, Sierra and I get together a couple of times a month, sometimes with another friend. If you like, you can join us." She says, looking genuinely excited by the idea.

"That would be nice," I say, honestly. "I've never really had anyone to sit at home and play games with. It was never my parents' thing." Spending time with me was never my parents' thing, regardless of what we were doing.

She looks at me with an expression I can't place and opens her mouth to speak, but as she does, there is a knock at the door. She rushes to the door and opens it. "Well, speak of the devil!"

She moves aside to let someone in and says, "I hope you don't mind, Nate. I invited Sierra over. Cleaning out my grandmother's room will be a big job, and, if I am being totally honest, it will be hard for me. I figured, why not have *both* my best friends here for it?"

My stomach churns. This day is already stressful, and now I have to meet someone new. "Sounds good to me," I lie.

My mind goes quiet as I watch the girl enter the apartment. She is brighter than the sun. She prances in like she is as light as a feather, her reddish blonde hair sliding over her shoulder as she tilts her head to the side and smiles at me.

"It's nice to meet you!" She says with so much enthusiasm that I nearly can't respond.

"Nice to meet you too," I say, my voice cracking.

I look over her shoulder and see Rex staring me in the eyes with her hand over her mouth, trying to stifle her laughter.

"Uh. Excuse me. I have to talk to Rex—I mean Quinn about, uh, roommate stuff." I grab Rex by the arm and haul her to the kitchen.

The kitchen is long but narrow. It's probably fine for one person to cook in, but navigating the kitchen with two people trying to prepare a meal would be complicated.

"What are you doing?" I whisper.

"What do you mean?" she asks with a smirk on her lips and a gleam in her eye.

"I know that face. You are scheming. You knew damn well this would happen." I say.

"I knew what would happen? I had no idea my beautiful, talented, funny, and totally available friend would turn you into a croaking frog."

"A croaking frog?"

"I heard your voice crack." She smirks at me.

"That just happens sometimes. It has nothing to do with her. I'm cool. I'm completely fine." I can feel my face heating.

"Then why did you feel the need to drag me to the kitchen for this talk? Hmm?"

I peer to the side, trying to think of a decent response when she speaks again.

"Whatever. You're cool. She's cool. I'm cool. Let's get started." She spins around quickly and returns to Sierra. I clear my throat, take a few deep breaths, and return to the living room as well.

* * *

Five hours later, I am seated on the couch, which is exactly as comfortable as it looked. Two boxes of pizza, a cookie pie, and a two-liter bottle of soda are spread out on the coffee table. Rex takes a seat on the opposite end of the couch and covers her legs with one of the many blankets while Sierra takes a spot on the teal armchair.

When we began clearing it out, my new bedroom was mostly clean, if not a bit dusty. It was very obviously the room of an older woman. There were a few pieces of old furniture that had once been in the living room and boxes upon boxes of old collectibles, jewelry, and photographs.

It didn't take much time to move the furniture to the storage unit Rex was now renting downstairs. What took the most time was sorting through the woman's boxes. Some things went straight to the trash, like old birthday cards from people Rex had never heard of and faded receipts. She allowed herself to keep a small container of her grandmother's belongings, but everything else went to the storage unit.

There were a few awkward moments when Sierra and I sat in the living room in silence, when Rex wanted to grieve in private. There were other times when Rex wanted to laugh and reminisce about the good times she spent with her Medzmama, so we sat with her while she talked and sometimes cried.

In the end, she kept a stack of letters she found that were written between her mother and grandmother, a handful of photographs, a long pearl necklace, and a crocheted blanket. She also moved a couple of items into the living room. She placed a blue teapot on the bookshelf and a stuffed rabbit on her computer desk.

Once the room was clear, I brought in my bags and the new mattress I had delivered here this morning. Once I made the bed with my new set of bedding and hung the curtains I purchased this morning, it began to feel like my own room. I decided to order a dresser as well, so I will be living out of my suitcase until it arrives, but I don't mind.

There is no room for my computer desk in the room, but with a bit of finesse, we made space in the living room by scooting Rex's desk over to the wall and pushing the bookshelf right up against it. My desk is pressed against the other side of the bookshelf, right next to the front door. It is a tight fit, but it works.

Throughout the day, I learned a bit more about Rex. Apparently, her grandmother was Armenian and had only moved to the United States a few years ago. She passed away last year and left everything to Rex. Rex's mother passed away when she was a freshman in high school, and her father is no longer in her life. I am not sure if he is dead or not. I have no plans to ask about him anytime soon. It seems like a touchy subject, and I am not one to impose on someone who is already doing me such a massive favor. I am living here for free after all.

This day has been exhausting, and I am gratified to finally settle in and enjoy my first meal in my new home.

"You are exactly how Quinn described you," Sierra says, looking tired but pleased. Her rusty gold hair, now tied in a messy ponytail, slips over her shoulder as she selects a slice of pizza.

"Ouch." I chuckle sarcastically.

She waves her hands in front of her. "No! No! I mean that in a good way! She told me you were a funny and kind person."

"Aw shucks," I say and playfully shove Rex on the shoulder.

She only rolls her eyes and takes another bite of her pepperoni and pineapple pizza.

I turn back to Sierra. "I'll admit, I don't know all that much about you. Rex has been very private about her life. Hell, I didn't even know she was a woman until a few weeks ago. How long have you two been friends?"

"Quinn and I have known each other since elementary school, but we hated each other at first. She was always a bit, uh, rough." She bites her lip and glances at her friend nervously. Quinn shrugs as if she already knew. "She and I became inseparable in middle school. It was about that time we realized that I made up for what she lacked and vice versa."

Rex groaned, "You pranced around like a damn fairy. I swear, anytime I left your house after a sleepover, I would have glitter falling off me for a week straight."

"It was better than your gloomy, baggy sweater-wearing ass practically hissing at people in the school hallways," retorted Sierra. She cleared her throat. "Anyway, Nate, we have been friends for so long that we have seen many different versions of each other. We had a couple of lost years when—"

Rex interrupts her mid-sentence with a click of her tongue and shakes her head.

Sierra continues, "—but we found each other again. And we *both* leveled out a bit. I don't use quite as much glitter anymore."

"But I still wear the baggy sweaters." Rex quips.

"That's true." Sierra shrugs and squeezes her friend's hand. "But you are so much happier than you were back then."

I look between the two girls. They share something invaluable: a friendship that has lasted through many years and struggles. I try not to dwell too long on Sierra's mention of *lost years* and just revel in the feeling of freedom. This is my life now, and I am so thankful. I am thankful to be out of my father's house. I am thankful that these kind, beautiful women are in my life now, that *this* is my life now.

"So!" Sierra says, and she nearly jumps from her seat, "Who wants to get their ass kicked at trivia?"

I stand up too and smirk right at her. "Oh, that challenge is accepted. You may have just met your match, Glitter Girl."

* * *

After the first hour of trivia, Rex excuses herself to work at her computer. I had never asked about her work, so I was curious and couldn't help but glance at her screen now and then out of curiosity.

Based on the glances I snagged when I was drawing my card or grabbing another piece of the cookie pie, it seems like she does a lot of typing and scrolling. So, just like every other online job out there.

Sierra clears her throat and hits me with a narrow, annoyed expression. "Nate! Did you hear me?"

"Jesus, you are mean when you get competitive. You were a docile lamb all day, and as soon as we pull out *Trivia Quest*, you become a vicious badger."

"Oh, like you are one to talk! Ugh, I'll just read it again." She pops her pointer and middle knuckles and then her wrists. "How many stones is the fairytale princess castle made of?"

"None," I say confidently. "It is a steel frame covered in concrete. It is just made to look like stone."

She stares at me with a flat expression. "Woohoo. You win, showoff. You know, you only had to say '*none.*' You didn't have to say what it was actually made of."

I grin at her, "Oh, come on, let me show off a bit. Nobody

plays trivia with me."

"I can see why," Rex says, turning in her desk chair. "Nobody plays with her either. I'm sure you can see why. As much as I enjoy seeing the two of you at each other's throats, would you mind moving *this...*" she says, waving her hand at the space between us, "...to the other room?"

Any words I wanted to say get stuck in my throat. Just the thought of being alone in my bedroom with this girl, really any girl other than Rylee, ties my stomach in a knot.

"No worries!" Sierra says cheerfully, already moving on from her brutal defeat, "I should get going anyway." She gives Rex a quick hug, then moves to the door. Before shutting the door behind her, she turns to me, "Enjoy your first night of freedom!" Then points at our friend, "You! Don't do anything dumb." She looks back at me, "You! Tell me if this one gives you trouble!"

"I will do that," I say with a nervous chuckle. I still don't know what to expect from Rex as a roommate. Do I need to worry about her giving me trouble?

"Goodbye, you two," Sierra sings as she shuts the door behind her.

"Well, she is enthusiastic," I say to Rex, who has already turned back around to resume her work. "I can tell she has rubbed off on you."

"What can I say? She filled my life with pixie dust. It's impossible to wash that shit off." Rex says, sounding annoyed, but in the glow of her monitor, I can see her smiling.

* * *

195

After a couple of hours of my usual evening activities of gaming and anime, I say goodnight to Rex and go to my new bedroom. I curl up on the new mattress and wrap myself in the sheets I chose for myself. It felt much more comfortable than any one billion thread count Egyptian cotton sheets my mother special-ordered. Despite the bedroom being one-third the size of my old room, it feels free and open. The heaviness I usually feel at the end of the day is nowhere to be found.

I fall into a quiet, heavy sleep and don't dream at all.

* * *

A slight sensation of panic hits my chest when I open my eyes. It takes a moment to remember where I am, but I quickly recall that I am meant to be here.

I glance at my phone. I have one unread message from my mother.

Your dad told me you are moving out. What happened?

Without responding, I hit the button to black out the screen. When I sit up, I notice I *desperately* need to take a piss.

I throw on my sweatpants and shirt as quickly as possible and rush into the hallway. The sound of the shower running stops me in my tracks. That is when the realization hit me. I have to share a bathroom.

At my parents' house, I had my own toilet just a few steps from my bed. I could roll out of bed naked, piss, and then fall back into bed without donning clothes or worrying about running into anyone else. I suppose my nude trips to the bathroom in the middle of the night are done. Not only do I have to worry about clothes when I use the toilet now, but I also have to worry about whether or not the bathroom will even be available. There were five and a half restrooms in my parents' house. I've never had to worry about this before.

One bathroom. One bathroom. SHIT I have to pee.

I knock on the door. "Rex. Are you almost done in there?"

"I'll just be a minute." She shouts back, sounding completely unhurried.

I take her word for it and sit back on my bed. I play a game on my phone for a while. I bounce my leg up and down. Five more minutes pass, and the shower is *still* running.

I knock again. "Rex! You said it would be a minute, five minutes ago!"

"I'll just be a minute!" She yells, unhurried, and now slightly annoyed.

I pace back and forth. Keep moving. Keep moving. I hop in place. Keep moving. Keep moving.

I sit on my bed again and cross my legs. I try to pass the time by playing a game again. Three more minutes pass, and I hear the water shut off. *Fucking finally.* I play the game for a few more minutes, waiting for her to come out, until I feel like my bladder is about to burst. I shout, "Quinn! What is taking so long? I have to piss like a fucking horse."

She shouts, "I'll just be a damn minute!"

After a few more minutes of pacing, I hear the bathroom door open. I jolt up and shove my way past her into the small bathroom. I shut the door a bit too aggressively, stand over the toilet, and *finally* relieve myself.

Once my business is done, I find Rex in the kitchen, pouring herself a bowl of cereal. "I'm sorry for yelling before. I had to pee. Like *really* bad."

"That's okay. Sorry if I took a long time. I'm not used to sharing a bathroom."

197

"Neither am I," I say, putting my head in my hands. I try to push back my annoyance, but the annoyance wins. "What the hell took so long?"

"Well, I have to wash my face, shampoo, condition, shave, exfoliate, then wash." She says, counting on her fingers like she is doing a tally of her tasks. "Once I am out of the shower, I have to put on my face serum and moisturizer, apply an oil and a cream to my hair, and then moisturize my body."

I stare at the kitchen floor and rub my temples, trying not to imagine her in a steamy shower or rubbing lotions on herself. "And it takes this long every time?"

"Well, I don't wash my hair every day, but pretty much, yeah."

This is going to be harder than I thought.

17

Balance

At least until Monday, I plan on doing absolutely nothing. I have some money and some time. I may as well take some of that time to enjoy being away from my father's suffocating grasp. I'm free.

"Nate!" I hear Rex howl from the kitchen.

I pause the show I've been watching and shout, "What's up?"

"Why are these dishes in the sink?"

I glance up from my plate of scrambled eggs and toast. "You mean what are the dishes I literally just used to cook my breakfast doing in the sink?" I press play, assuming that is all that needs to be said.

"Oh. Never mind. Can you clean them up when you are done with your food?"

I groan and pause the show I was watching again. "Of course I will, Quinn." I can cut her some slack. She doesn't know my habits yet, after all.

Rex bounds for the door in her running shorts, sports bra, and (surprise, surprise) an unzipped hoodie that is two sizes too large.

"When did you start calling me Quinn?" She says with a wink.

"Don't get hit by a car, Rex," I say, rolling my eyes and pressing play again.

Two hours later, Rex returns, sweating, with her hoodie now tied around her waist. "You're still on your computer?"

"What? Are you my mother? I thought I left my parents' house." I gesture to my monitor. "Yes, I am still on my computer. Fuck off."

She grunts and rolls her eyes, but indeed fucks off to take a shower, once again taking an entire hour to do so.

When she returns, she sits at her computer to begin her workday. Neither of us says another word until dinner.

* * *

The next two days go almost just the same. I wake up late, eat, play games, eat again, and play more games.

Rex runs to the gym, comes back home, then works for a couple of hours on what I eventually learn are graphic design gigs. She plays games until dinner. After dinner, she reads and is usually in bed by ten.

On Friday, before Rex begins her work, she asks me to pause my game.

"I've invited some friends over tonight to play board games. You can play with us if you like, but if you don't, that's fine too."

I shrug, "No worries. I've got headphones. You won't bother me."

"That's what I figured. I'm not sure what we're playing yet, but Hayden and Sierra will be here at 7:00. "

I take off my headphones and place them on the desk. "Actually, I think I will play with you guys."

A slow, devious smile forms on her lips. "That's what I thought."

Ignoring her obvious scheming, I say, "I'll make everyone dinner," as I get up from my chair.

I quickly dress and make my way to the store to buy ingredients to make roasted chicken, potatoes, and carrots. On the way, I debate buying ingredients for brownies as well, but opt to buy a platter of cookies from a bakery instead.

Once I return home, I get to work on prepping the chicken. I melt butter on the stove with fresh herbs: parsley, sage, rosemary, and thyme. I strain the infused butter and use the cooking syringe I just purchased to inject the chicken with the butter. Just like Grace taught me. I coat the bird in olive oil, spread the buttery herbs over the skin, and sprinkle the whole thing with a hefty coating of salt and pepper.

I prepare the potatoes and carrots, then add them to the baking dish once the bird is halfway done cooking. I slice a loaf of bread and place it along with some butter on a dish next to the platter of cookies.

Cooking tonight for friends feels different than cooking for myself. I find myself in a peaceful state, flowing through the small kitchen, learning the locations of all the pans and utensils as I go.

By the time the meal is done, Hayden and Sierra arrive.

We pile into the small living room and, after a bit of discussion, decide to play *Pilgrims of Dalon*.

Through a mouthful of her food, Sierra asks, "You made this, Nate?"

"I did," I say, feeling slightly insecure. I've never cooked for anyone but myself and Grace.

"It's amazing!"

I blush, but try to sound smooth as I say, "Thanks. It's not much. Sometimes the simplest foods can be the most satisfying." I cut myself off before I can sound too pretentious.

She nods at me, taking another bite of her meal.

"If you cook every night, I will give you a discount on your rent and pay for half the cost of the ingredients," Rex says, with a semi-wild expression on her usually cool face.

I raise my eyebrows and cackle, stopping abruptly. "Hell no."

The whole room laughs, and a feeling of warmth and belonging that I have never felt so strongly fills my chest.

Once the laughter subsides, Hayden chimes in, "You're looking for a job, right? Why not be a chef?"

I consider for a moment. It would be nice to experience the peace I felt tonight every day, but I was cooking for friends. I don't think it would feel the same cooking for strangers. Plus, I would have to rush to get the food out, and that would make me so damn anxious. So I respond, "Because I *enjoy* cooking. Having time restrictions and doing it all day long would take all the fun out of it for me," I say.

"That's fair." He shrugs. "I guess everyone doesn't want to do their hobbies for a living."

I look around the room. Everyone else in this room did just that. Rex made a career out of art. Sierra makes a living wage as a singer. Hayden plans to make a career out of surfing, a hobby he can no longer enjoy, at least not in the same way. And I have no idea what to do. I've moved away, but I am nowhere near being a real adult. I have no plans. I have no goals. I can feel myself sinking into that familiar pit once more; the feeling of hopelessness stirring back to life in my chest.

Rex's eyes land on me, and she immediately hops up from

her seat. "Let's get the game started!" She says as she collects everyone's plates and brings them to the kitchen.

The change of topic has me snapping out of my funk and unboxing the game. I challenge my friends, "Are you ready for the worst beat down you've had in your life?"

"Are you kidding?" Sierra scoffs, "I'm going to be the one kicking your asses up and down Dalon."

And she did.

Around ten o'clock, our game had ended. Hayden went home, and Rex withdrew to her bedroom, leaving Sierra and me on the couch alone.

She was the one who broke the slightly awkward silence. "I had a lot of fun playing with you tonight. I haven't met many people who can match my competitive spirit."

I laugh, "*Competitive spirit*? Is that what you call it? I'd call it being aggressively zealous."

"Whatever you want to call it, you match it, so you are just as deranged as I am." She grins at me in a way that makes my whole body tighten.

Rylee's grin lingers in the back of my mind. I push away the guilt that pulses through me. No. Rylee has moved on, if that's what you would call it in this bizarre situation. There is no reason to feel guilty for being attracted to another woman.

I take a deep breath, letting the feelings pass, and suggest, "Well, I still have some *competitive spirit* left in me. We could play something else. How about a little trivia rematch?"

She smiles and moves to retrieve *Trivia Tussle* from the top shelf. I resist the urge to check her out as she stretches to reach for the box.

I fail.

She is taller than Rylee, and her body is curvier than the petite dancer's build I'm used to. I manage to pull my gaze from her ass before she turns back around.

After three rounds of trivia, Sierra says it is time for her to go. I walk her to her car and wave goodbye as she pulls out of the parking lot. I linger on the sidewalk, shove my hands in the pockets of my sweatpants, and stare at the night sky.

* * *

I spend the weekend and the next two days exactly how I spent the week, but on Wednesday, my day of playing games and fucking off is cut short when it is time for me to go to my weekly appointment with Dr. Reggie. It's my first appointment since I was discharged from the hospital, and I am dreading it.

I take extra care to make myself look like I am completely and totally fine. I style my hair a bit more carefully and choose my least wrinkled shirt from my newly assembled dresser. I look into my bedroom mirror, which once belonged to Rex's Medzmama. I am surprised but glad to see the circles under my eyes are mostly gone, and my skin looks brighter. I've been sleeping better this week than I have in a very long time.

I haven't been getting drunk since I moved here. Granted, I can't buy alcohol as a nineteen-year-old, and I didn't steal any from my parents' house, but I also haven't felt much desire to drink. I still have moments when I think to myself, "*Damn, a drink would be good right now,*" but I don't feel like I *have* to drink to get through the day anymore. That probably lends to my clearer skin and better sleep.

I grab my phone, wallet, and house key, then say a quick goodbye to Rex, who has already started working.

The bus ride and the waiting room feel the same as last

week. I don't know why I expected everything to be completely different today. I guess it's like when you leave for vacation and return home. You expect things to be different, to *feel* different. Only this vacation was a failed suicide attempt and a hospital stay, not a relaxing getaway.

"Nathan." Dr. Reggie says in an even tone on the other side of the door that separates the waiting room from all the offices.

"Nate," I say, "Good afternoon, Doc."

"I apologize. I'll have to remember that Nate is your preferred name."

"It's alright. Nathan is my father, *or* what my father would call me when he was pissed." I give him a half smile as if to say it's not all that serious.

We complete the rest of the short walk to his office in a calm silence, although I can feel a tightening sensation in my chest. He has to know. I requested that the records from my hospital visit be sent to him. Not so he knows all the medical nitty-gritty of my extended visit, but to spare me the misery of having to explain to him everything that happened.

I take a seat on that familiar sofa as Dr. Reggie sits in his desk chair and spins to face me, stylus poised to take detailed notes on his tablet.

"You tried to kill yourself." He looks at me with a flat expression, looking for confirmation.

I only offer a slight nod.

"Tell me what happened."

Well, fuck me. I pause before responding, "Didn't you get the records from the hospital?"

"I did, but I need you to tell me exactly what happened. The hospital notes are basic. Their concerns are medical, and the psychological portion is, well, lacking. I need to hear it from you. Your own words. From the triggering moment to now."

I swallow hard and dive headfirst into my story, exactly how I saw it, exactly how it felt.

"I met with my ex, Rylee."

Dr. Reggie's posture changes when I mention her. I can tell he remembers Rylee from our first session together.

"We met for coffee. She wanted to explain why she broke up with me and why she was so mean when she did it. She broke up with me, not because she was embarrassed by me or thought I wasn't good enough, but because she is a lesbian." I look up at him, and he is nodding in confirmation that he heard, but says nothing. I take that as a signal to continue.

"I was relieved. I could accept that. It wasn't about me at all. She was finding herself during our relationship and wanted to be honest and fair with me when she knew for sure who she was."

I pause for a long moment, rubbing a cold hand on my knee. "What I couldn't accept was what I saw after. I don't think she was trying to flaunt it; as a matter of fact, I'm pretty sure she thought I couldn't see her. But I did. I saw her kiss her best friend, who I suppose is probably her girlfriend. She has been friends with Ashley almost as long as she has been friends with me. Before I could think better of it, our whole relationship felt like a lie. I imagined harbored feelings and infidelity that had been going on for *years.* I remember all the times Ashe seemed jealous of me. I remember all the times she was controlling of Rylee. I already felt like dying before, but now I felt like the only good thing about my life was a fallacy."

I told the doctor of the despair, the hopelessness, and the strange clarity I felt before my quick decision to end my life. It was the easiest decision I had ever made. That's when the sudden truth hit me, that I would be successful this time because, this time, I was ready. I wanted it more than anything. This time, there would be no going back. But I was forced back by the miracle of modern medicine.

I let him in on the horrible things my father said to me. I tell him about the friends who visited me in the hospital and about moving in with Rex.

This is the first time I have admitted out loud that I don't know if I'm glad I made it through, but I do know my life is moving in an unpredictable direction. I don't know where the hell I am going, but I want to stay alive to find out what happens next. Like, my life is now my new favorite book, and I am simply staying alive for the plot.

When I finish my story, Dr. Reggie finally responds, "Whatever it is that is keeping you here on Earth with us, hold on to it. Whether it is a person, a hobby, or just for the mystery and suspense of life itself, do not let it go. Now, you said you need to find a job. How is that going?"

"I've been applying for jobs, but nobody wants to hire me. The term 'entry level' is a damned dirty lie."

"Have you tried lowering your standards and expectations? You could accept something less than you are qualified for to gain general work experience."

I sit back, suddenly feeling less invested in the conversation. "My standards are literally the lowest they could be."

"My advice would be to take advantage of the grace period Rex has given you and the funds you currently have. Take a few months if you have to. Find something you love. Find a passion and pursue it. You can live a happy, fulfilling life. I am sure of it."

"No offense, doctor, but that sounds much easier said than

done."

"That may be true. Now is the time to accept that challenge. The answer is most likely right in front of you. What is it you already enjoy doing? How could you make a career out of it?" He glances at the clock hanging next to the door. "Unfortunately, that's all the time we have for today. If you require another session before our next scheduled one, check in with the front desk or call my office phone. You are meant to be here with us. Do not hesitate to reach out if you think of attempting suicide again. I look forward to seeing you next week."

I stand and glance back at him as I open the door. "I'll see you next week, Doc."

He gives me a reassuring nod and smile.

I walk back out onto the city sidewalk feeling lighter than I have in a very, very long time. I return to my apartment to find that Rex had left for her lunch date with Hayden, so I have the entire place to myself. I could play a game with no interruptions, but I walk past my computer and lie on my bed instead.

I stare at the ceiling. I suppose it is time for me to start looking at my life more seriously. I need to find a job. I need to find a purpose. I need to earn my keep.

What do I want to do with my life?

The question doesn't feel overwhelming like it did when I lived at my father's house. I don't need to impress anyone. I don't need to have a grand plan for my future. My future is *mine,* and I decide what I make of it. For now, I simply want to survive.

* * *

I'm an hour into punching zombies when Rex returns.

"You are *still* on your computer."

"I've only been on for an hour," I say, annoyed. Who the hell does she think she is?

"You were on your computer all morning, too. That time still counts."

"Are you really one to talk? You are on your computer all afternoon!"

She huffs and crosses her arms. "*I* have balance in my life. I run every morning, go to the gym three times a week, attend a boxing class once a week, and meet with a friend at least twice a week. My afternoons on my computer are spent not only playing, but also working. *You* lounge in bed until at least 10 a.m. and play on your computer all day."

I roll my eyes. "What *should* I be doing, then?"

"Come run with me tomorrow."

"I haven't run since my sophomore year of high school. Also, I have pulmonary fibrosis, Rex! I can't run until my pulmonologist clears me."

"Well, try a different hobby then." Rex turns, grabs one of her massive fantasy novels off the bookshelf, and tosses it to me. "Try this. I think you'll like this one."

I catch the book. "I thought you would be a cool roommate."

She stares at me and taps her foot. "I am trying to be a good friend. I don't want to see you get in a rut. I am *trying* to look out for you."

I roll my eyes, but flip the novel over to read the back cover. Much to my dismay, it sounds damn interesting. I shut down my game and stand from my chair.

I plop onto the teal armchair and glare at her. "I'll give it a shot."

* * *

I don't put the book down for three hours. I am only dragged away from the pages by the incessant growling of my stomach.

After I finish eating a quick meal of microwaved leftovers, I grab the book from where I returned it to the shelf. I take my spot on the teal chair, joining Rex for her usual after-dinner reading time.

Before I have the chance to open my book, Rex looks up from her book and says, "You remember Drew, right?"

Drew. The pot dealer who refuses to use my real name. "Yeah, I remember him," I confirm.

"I haven't talked much about him, but we are actually pretty good friends. I know you have mixed feelings about him, but would you mind if I invited him and his boyfriend over for dinner on Friday?"

Despite my near aversion to the man, I look forward to having an excuse to make another meal. "Why not? I have a pot roast recipe Grace gave me that I have been wanting to try."

She looks at me with an almost guilty expression. "I didn't mean to make it sound like I was *expecting* you to cook. I just wanted to run it by you because this is your home, too. I didn't want you to be blindsided. If you want to cook, I'll spot you some money for the meal."

"It's not a problem. I'll take you up on the cash, though." I wink at her and open my book.

We spend the next two hours reading our books in a silent, peaceful apartment.

* * *

The doorbell rings at ten till seven. I didn't expect Drew to be the type to arrive early, but I've certainly read people wrong before.

Thankfully, Rex, who I've learned is rarely on time for *anything*, was ready early for once and was there to greet him and his boyfriend, Peter.

I begin to set the table and hear Rex exclaim, "Hey, guys!" as she opens the door.

I hear a murmur of hellos and then Rex's voice saying, "Come say hello to my new roomie!"

"Cookie Man!"

I look up to see Drew beaming and coming at me with open arms. He grips me in a too-familiar hug.

"Hey, man," I manage to get out despite his bone-crushing squeeze.

He lets go of me and turns to Rex, "You said you had a roommate, but you never said it was Cookie Man!"

"I didn't realize you two were so close." With a puzzling look in my direction, she asks, "Cookie Man?"

"It's a long story. We can talk about it over dinner." I feel anxious, but relieved that we will at least have the meal to serve as a distraction. "Let's eat."

We all sit down at the table, where Drew introduces me to Peter. With dark skin and long hair, he looks like the exact opposite of Drew. Like any good guests, they compliment the meal and thank me for preparing it.

"So, Cookie Man is more than just cookies, huh?"

"Of course. I didn't even make those cookies I gave you, though."

"But he makes some damn good chocolate chip cookies," Rex says. "So you gave him cookies?" She says, pointing at Drew with her fork.

"Oh, you never told her the story?" Drew says, looking genuinely surprised and slightly insulted. "I thought our fated meeting made more of an impression than that. Here I thought we had a connection written in the stars. Two spirits destined to cross paths and make a profound difference in each other's lives."

Peter smirks and shakes his head, "Stop fucking around, Drew."

I look back and forth between the two men sitting across from me. This is why I have mixed feelings about this guy. He is unpredictable. I never know what to say to him. I look back at Rex, expecting her to say something, but she appears just as perplexed as I am. Then, to my relief, Drew tells the story of how we met, along with the story of our second chance encounter. Rex seems enthralled by his tale the entire time.

Over the course of the meal, I realize that not only does Peter look like the exact opposite of Drew, but he also has an opposite personality. Despite this, they flow in a perfectly complementary way. They balance each other, and I find myself enjoying their company.

We come to the end of our meal, and I finally get up the nerve to ask, "So, you sell marijuana?"

Rex verified my suspicions while we were having coffee one day. She told me she met Drew through a mutual friend, and she uses marijuana to help her relax when she feels anxious or to calm her mind when her bad memories haunt her.

Drew smiles and, in a matter-of-fact tone, says, "Yes, Cookie Man, that is my profession."

"Why do you bother in a state where recreational use is legal?"

"Ah," he says, wagging his finger, "but it is only legal to those 21 and older."

"So you sell to minors?" I ask, trying not to sound too accusatory.

"I don't sell to minors. I sell to those between the ages of 18 and 21."

"Why?"

He shrugs, "Because I think the law is stupid. Some states allow medical use to 18-year-olds. Hell, some allow it to minors. And the shit they sell there is the same shit we have here. If 18, 19, and 20-year-olds can benefit from it medically, why shouldn't they have it here in a state where it is legal for recreational use?"

I sit back in my chair, silently considering his point. I grew up in a house where I learned that using pot makes you a bad person and leads to worse drugs. It's not like my mother was one to talk, considering her pill addiction.

Drew continues, "I used to never leave my house. I tried to convince my mom to let me be home-schooled because there were days when I would get physically ill thinking of going to school. I was absent often and began falling behind in my classes. I didn't go to college because of it. My mother couldn't tell me what was going on with me. I thought I was crazy. I finally saw a therapist when I left home at 21 years old. She told me I had severe anxiety. I was reluctant to try traditional medication, so she mentioned marijuana could be effective for me. When I tried it, it changed my life. I could calm my mind *and* my stomach. I could leave my house. I am in college now, and this profession covers my tuition plus some. I'm happy to be helping people like me find their peace. If I could have tried this three years earlier, I would be three years ahead."

I found myself staring at Drew intently, leaning with my elbows on the table, my clasped hands resting on my chin. I realize he and I might have more in common than I thought.

I nod, "I can respect that." I sit back in my chair again. "Does anyone have room for dessert?"

Both Rex and Peter recline in their chairs, placing their hands on their abdomens, looking like they may burst if they eat another bite.

Drew smirks and places three gummies on the table, one of which he cuts in half. He slides one half to Rex and the other to me and says, "We will soon."

18

Hopeful

I'm almost two weeks into living on my own, and it feels hopeless. I've applied for job after job. Host work, waiting tables, cleaning hotel rooms; all hiring managers say the same thing: no experience, no job. My high school diploma is worthless, no matter how prestigious the school is. At this rate, I will be on my knees in front of my father begging him to let me live in his home again after the money he gave me runs out.

I can't let that happen. I am done with that life. I refuse to answer to that horrible man again.

That is how I ended up here, leaning against the picket fence in front of my parents' house at 7:50 a.m. on a Wednesday. I stare straight ahead at the road, barely glancing at the house once since I walked from the bus stop twenty minutes ago.

I hear the rumble and squeak of Marty's truck before I see it. A lump forms in my throat. I gulp, trying to prepare myself for what I am about to ask. Whether it is a favor or an offer, I don't know.

My upper lip begins to sweat as he pulls into the drive. I can see the surprise on his face before he even turns off the engine.

"G'morning, Nate," Marty says as he shuts the door to his truck.

"Hey, Marty. How have you been?"

"I can't complain." He says as he makes his way to the gate. He offers no follow-up question and looks at me expectantly.

I rub the back of my neck. "Um. Marty." I pause and let my mind calm. Despite rehearsing what I planned to say repeatedly before he arrived, I struggle to get the words out. "Have you ever considered hiring any help?"

He half smiles, "I've thought about it a few times. My days are rather full, and I have had to deny a few contracts that would take up too much of my time without help." There is a pause, and when he noticed I wasn't going to speak immediately, he inquired, "Why do you ask?"

"As you know, I am living on my own. Well, not technically alone. I am living with a friend, but I have to pay my own way now. And I need a job. Nobody wants a private school boy with no work experience." Sensing I am rambling, I clear my throat and try to make my point. "I really enjoyed working with you. I'd like to work with you again. On all the jobs, I mean."

"Hmm," Marty hums to himself, considering. "You know, Nate, I had dreams of making this a family business, once. There was a point in my life when I was married."

I raise my eyebrows a little bit out of shock, but mostly out of curiosity. Marty and I had spent many hours over the last few weeks sharing stories, but he never mentioned a wife. I just assumed he had never been married.

"My wife and I had a boy. His name was Nick." Marty bows his head slightly, diverting his gaze. "When he was 17 years old, he died from a brain tumor. He wanted to work with me, but those dreams were shattered once we were told he wouldn't live much longer. My marriage crumbled, too. Losing a child can do that to a marriage, no matter how 'in love' you are."

"I am so sorry to hear that, Marty. I didn't mean to open up a wound. Forget that I asked. I will find something else." I turn to walk down the sidewalk, but Marty begins to speak again, halting me in my tracks.

"His 26th birthday was last week." Marty finally raises his head. "I think he would be glad for me to take this step. I think he would want me to take on a new apprentice and grow my business. *Our* family business."

I turn back to him but say nothing.

"Yes, Nate, I would like your help. I'd like to accept the bigger contracts. I've seen you work. You have a talent for this, and I see how at peace you are with it. It reminds me of myself. It reminds me of Nick. If I were to hire anyone to help make Nick's dream a reality, it would be you."

My heartbeat quickens from the excitement. "I won't let you down, Marty! I can be here early and work as late as you need. I can bring lunch and coffee and—"

"Whoa, hold on there, Nate. I don't have the contracts for full-time yet, but I can take you on part-time and increase your hours once I secure more clients. What do you say to..." He trails off as if doing calculations in his head, "...twenty dollars an hour?"

That is certainly more than Taco Squire would pay me. "I'll take it!" I can barely hold back my excitement.

"I'm glad to have you on my team then." Marty gives me a big, genuine smile and a firm handshake. "You can start tomorrow. I'll have some formal paperwork drawn up, and I will pick you up from your apartment at six in the morning. For obvious reasons, I don't think it would be wise to let you work at your old house, but you can work with me on all the other morning jobs, and I will drop you back off at your apartment when I usually break for lunch."

I bounce on my toes, suppressing the urge to jump up and down like an excited schoolgirl. "That sounds perfect, Marty. Thank you. *Thank* you!"

"Well, go home and enjoy your last day as a young man with no responsibilities. Tomorrow, I'll put you to work."

"Yes, sir," I say with a smile and begin walking to the bus stop. I don't turn to look at my parents' house once.

* * *

I burst through the front door and find Rex, hair wet from her morning shower, munching on cereal at her desk. "I did it! I got the job!"

She puts down her bowl, lurches from her seat, and throws her arms around me. "Yes! I knew it was a good idea! Congratulations, Nate!"

I pull back from the hug. "Thank you for suggesting it. I wouldn't have even given it a shot if it weren't for you."

"I remember the first time you worked with Marty. It was the first time you seemed even a little alive after everything with Rylee."

I begin walking back and forth in our living room, feeling full of energy. "Something about the work makes me feel alive. Moving my body, sweating, whatever it is, makes me feel peaceful."

"I'm happy for you. You still don't have to pay for three months, though. I really don't mind."

"As soon as I get my first paycheck, I will pay this month's rent."

Rex pats me on the shoulder with a smile and sits down to finish her breakfast.

I feel like a real person for the first time in a very long time. Yes, moving out of my parents' house was huge, but I have never provided for myself. I have never relied upon only myself. And I feel free.

I sit at my desk to enjoy my last day as a boy with no responsibilities. Tomorrow, I am a man who can provide for himself.

* * *

My day of being a "boy with no responsibilities" is cut short when I realize it is almost time for my weekly meeting with Dr. Reggie. I don't feel any pressure to look like everything is fine today, but I try to look decent regardless.

Despite the afternoon rain, I am in a cheerful mood. It doesn't feel like a dreary rain that makes you want to curl up and watch TV all day, but a rain that washes away stress and mental grime. The kind of cloudy, wet day you want to endure simply to smell the moisture in the air and stomp through the puddles like a child.

Although the women in the office seem the same as before, my mood makes the place feel lighter, and I can see in Dr. Reggie's face that he can feel it too when he calls me to his office.

"You seem a bit more cheerful today." He says with a grin.

"I got a job this morning," I say, smiling unabashedly.

"That is great news! What will you be doing?"

"I will be working with a friend, actually. He owns a small landscaping and handyman business. He hired me on as an apprentice."

When I say it out loud, I can feel my light dim as my thoughts shift to my father.

"What was that? You were so proud and excited a moment ago."

My eyes drop to my hands, now folded in my lap. "I was supposed to be an apprentice to my father. That's what he had planned for me. I can't help but wonder what he would think now. I took a job at another family business. I plan to do work that he would consider beneath him. He will think of me as an embarrassment."

"Does it truly matter what your father thinks? He said awful things to you in the hospital and well before that, by the sound of it."

"It matters because I have been told my entire life that it matters. Everyone thinks he is perfect. He has the perfect home and wife. I am the only disappointment. People look at me and think I am the black sheep. That I am the one who taints my family name."

"Let's face these thoughts. Let's break it down. Is your father perfect?"

"No. He is cheating on my mother, and I know there is more he is hiding from us. I just can't prove it."

"So no, he is not perfect. Are his home and wife really perfect?"

"His home is beautiful, but he is never there to enjoy it, which was honestly the only part I liked about living there. And my mom." I pause, hesitant to say anything bad against her. "She has a drug problem, and she was never really there for me. She pretended to be, but it wasn't genuine."

"They are not perfect. Nobody and nothing really is. Are you really a disappointment?"

"My father would say I am."

"What do *you* say?"

"I don't know."

Dr. Reggie pauses for a moment, then continues, "What do you want out of your life?"

"I want to live it. I want to have people who care about me. I want to find something I enjoy doing. I don't want to ask for anything from anyone."

The therapist sits forward in his chair. "You have friends, old and new, and from the sound of it, they want the best for you. You just got a job you seem to be really excited about. You are living somewhere where you have the freedom to be yourself. So, let me ask the question a bit differently: are you a disappointment *to yourself* ?"

My heartbeat somehow feels faster and slower. "No. I am proud of myself." I can't help but smile, and neither can Dr. Reggie.

"Is there anything else new going on in your life?" He asks, leaning back in his chair.

"I think I am starting to have feelings for someone. It feels weird. I haven't dated. Not really. Rylee and I had been together for years, and it just sort of happened. We were pushed together. I'm thinking about asking this girl out, but I don't know what to do."

"It can be strange to develop feelings for someone new after a long relationship. Let it feel strange. Explore it. Be honest with yourself, and most importantly, if you decide to pursue this person, do not let the relationship become who you are.

Do not become too dependent. Nate is a great person. Don't lose him."

Even quicker than last week, the appointment is over. On my way home, I stop by a store to pick up some sturdy clothes and boots for my first day of work. When I return home, I go online to purchase my own phone plan, severing the final tie to my father's support.

* * *

I wake up with only 30 minutes to get ready for my day. I'm doing manual labor. It isn't like waking up early to shower would do me any good, so I give myself time to have a cup of tea (which became my morning ritual as soon as I saw Rex's electric kettle), get dressed, shave, apply deodorant, and brush my teeth. Starting tomorrow, I will give myself an extra ten minutes to eat breakfast. I woke up to a text from Marty specifically telling me not to eat this morning. That had me promptly hitting the snooze button.

I leave my room at the exact moment Rex leaves hers. She is already dressed to go for her morning run.

I give her a teasing grin. "I am so glad I will be at work while you hog the bathroom for three hours after your workout. I better not be paying for those extra-long showers."

She shoves my shoulder, "I don't recall seeing any money to begin with." She begins a steady jog to the door. "Good luck today!"

I grab my key, wallet, phone, and earbuds and follow her out the door with two minutes to spare before Marty should be pulling up to the curb. I admire his timeliness. It is something that we have in common.

As I reach the sidewalk at the front of the complex, Marty pulls up right in front of me. I hop in the passenger seat.

"Good morning, Nate," Marty says with a grin.

"Good morning, Marty. Where are we off to first?"

"First things first, we have to make this official. I have some paperwork for you to fill out. I figure we could take care of that over breakfast." He shifts the truck into drive.

"Sounds good to me." I have always been ravenous first thing in the morning. There is no way I could focus on work without a proper meal.

We arrive at a 24-hour diner and sit in the corner booth. I opt for the side next to the window so I can see the entire restaurant. After the waitress takes our drink orders—tea with sugar and milk for me, black coffee for him— he slides a small stack of paperwork to me.

"I just need you to fill out the bank drafting form, insurance paperwork, I-9, W-4, and a general employment agreement that states your wage, guaranteed weekly hours, and responsibilities."

I scan through the paperwork, signing and initialing where necessary. I was done before our drinks arrived.

We ordered our food and then began discussing the morning schedule. Most mornings, we have two houses to hit, except on Wednesday, when I will only be joining him for one of them. He invited me to a shared calendar, and I frowned as I scrolled through, looking at the names associated with each of the contracts. Some contracts belonged to families I had known since childhood, like Dominic's parents and the Fulton family. Thankfully, the Dunwalls' house is scheduled for the afternoon, so I won't have to go to Rylee's house, not for a while anyway.

Our food arrives, and I place my phone down. I expect to be

filled with nerves. I expect my appetite to vanish as soon as I look at my meal, but it doesn't. I don't feel dread or panic. It feels right.

I am looking forward to getting started. I'm looking forward to putting in my earbuds and falling into that flow I savored so much.

Once we finish our meal, Marty gives me a t-shirt and a water bottle with his business name printed on them. "You aren't required to wear the shirt, but you can if you like. Also, it is important to stay hydrated, especially if you aren't used to working in the heat for long hours."

I make a mental note to wear the shirt at least once a week and immediately fill the water bottle with the to-go water I got from the restaurant. It was a decent cup, not the kind of garbage you would get from a job fair, but an insulated one with a straw and a spill-proof top. The logo, however, was a bit plain.

Before I knew it, the day was done. The four hours of work went by too quickly, but it felt exhilarating to earn my own money for the first time in my life. Marty and I spent the morning taking turns mowing and detailing. There were some jobs I still didn't feel comfortable doing, like shaping rounded topiaries, but Marty insisted I could do it and made me try. He claimed that if it looked like shit, he would take the heat for me. It turned out much better than I expected.

* * *

I wake up the next morning, excited to get my day started. I crave the feelings of physical fatigue and satisfaction that come along with my work.

When I walk to the kitchen to make my cup of tea, I find Rex leaning against the counter, examining my new cup.

"What's your deal, Rex?" I ask as I hold out my hand to retrieve my property from her.

She looks at me eagerly, holding up the tumbler and pointing to the logo. "I could make something better. Marty is trying to get more work, right? A new logo could help stir up business. Is he running ads?"

"Are you light on work or something?"

She chuckles, "No, I have plenty of gigs lined up, but when I see crappy advertising, I get this all-consuming urge to make it better. I can't tell you how many files of logos I have saved on my computer that nobody actually hired me to do."

"I'd love to see them sometime, but I have to get to work." I've looked over Rex's shoulder a few times as she worked over the last couple of weeks. She occasionally asked for my opinion on color, spacing, or some other artist's terminology I have already forgotten. I never had anything to add, but it opened the designer's eye that my father tried to cultivate in me. She is an amazing artist and excellent at what she does. She has a zest for it that I think I am starting to understand.

I meet Marty in the same spot as yesterday.

"Good morning, Nate," he says once I am settled in my seat.

"Morning. This might seem like an odd question, but what are you doing to reel in more work?" I ask.

"I have a couple of people that I've had to say no to in the past. You might not have noticed, but I added them to the calendar last night. So I'll need you to work Monday afternoons starting next week."

"That's great, Marty! What about the other open time slots?"

"I suppose for the other afternoons, we will just be relying on word of mouth."

"Okay." I think back on Rex's offer. "Have you thought about advertising?"

"I put out some newspaper ads about 10 years ago."

I laugh, "Marty, I mean like social media. You can make a business page and pay to advertise on social media or post on local pages to publicize for free."

Marty hums, looking like he is considering my idea seriously. "I'm not good at that kind of thing."

"I can handle it." I shrug, "I have a friend who is a graphic designer. She could make a new logo and some advertisements that will really stand out."

"Oh. I don't know about that."

"She has already offered to help for free," I lie. I can pay for it myself to help out Marty. He has already done so much for me. "Just let her whip up a couple of designs and see how you feel about it."

He ponders a bit more, but by the time we arrive at the first house of the day, he says, "Okay. Your friend can handle the advertisements, and you can deal with the social media stuff. If it gets us seven more contracts, I will move you to full-time."

I smile, "Yes! This is going to be great. Who knows, maybe you will even have to expand; buy a new truck, hire another hand or two—"

"Alright, kid. Don't jump the gun," Marty interrupts as he turns off the truck, but he smiles, "get your ass to work."

I smile back at him and start unloading the equipment.

* * *

Thirty minutes into the first job of the day, I am tapped on the shoulder. I whirl, nearly slashing the intruder's leg with the weed eater. I turn off the machine and tug out an earbud. I look up and am horrified to see the face of Scotty Fulton. Right, this is his parents' house.

"Is this what you are doing now, Nate?"

"Is *this* what you are doing now, Scotty?" I gesture to his too-short running shorts. "Running around in your hot pants and living at your parents' house?"

He squares up slightly and sneers. "Oh, shut up. I heard your dad kicked you out."

"So what? I'm living unrestricted now, which is more than you can say," I say, jerking my head toward his parents' house.

"I also heard Rylee dumped you," he says with a smirk, completely ignoring my previous comment.

"Yeah, Rylee dumped me." I shrug, hiding my surprise at how little the statement hurts me, "Weren't you supposed to be first in line to fuck her? How is that going for you?" I lean on the picket fence with exaggerated ease.

His mouth twitches, and he glares. "You'll always be a loser, Nate." He shoves past me, walking toward the house.

I switch the weed eater back on. "And you will always be a dick."

* * *

"Oh, Rex!" I sing, channeling Grace. "I got you a new job!"

"Great! I had some free time today, so I decided to make a few mock-ups," she says as she turns toward her screen.

I lean over her, propping an arm on her desk. "You were that sure I would ask Marty about it, huh?"

"Yes, but it wasn't that. The all-consuming urge to improve

227

took over me."

"You are so damn dramatic." I laugh.

I examine her work: a new logo and a flier-style advertisement. "This is amazing, Rex. It's modern, but still very Marty."

The design was simple, but striking. Where most lawn care companies might use green, she used an array of colors. The only green in it was a strip of grass directly below an orange lawnmower. The silhouettes of Marty and me are positioned behind the mower; Marty's silhouette is standing with a hammer in his hand, and mine is holding a hedge trimmer. The entire design is surrounded by a sleek black circle with the name *"Marty's Home and Lawn Care"* printed in a classic and modest font at the bottom.

I send Marty the file, and he immediately responds, "Let's go for it."

19

My Story

In just my boxers, I sit on my bed using tweezers to carefully pick pills off the ugliest Christmas sweater I could find at the secondhand store down the road. At our last game night, Sierra made a bet that she would beat everyone else by at least 20 points. If she won, her prize was to make a request which none of us were allowed to deny. Well, she won by 26 points. Her request? An ugly sweater-themed Christmas Eve party.

Everyone else groaned when she made her request, but the excited sparkle in her eyes made me *want* to say yes to her, bet or no bet. Despite the horrific sweater, I want to look my best. I put on the nicest pair of jeans I own, and style my hair to the best of my abilities. Over the last few months, I've let it grow out, letting my curls fall onto my forehead and over my ears. My mother would've never let me go this long without a haircut. It suits me, though.

I step up to the full-length mirror to examine myself. I notice, for the first time, that I am starting to look like a man. I no longer look awkward and boyish. My skin is clear. I look less gangling, which is no doubt a benefit of working a physically demanding job. My shoulders look broader. I am carrying myself differently. It's like I am a completely different person than I was six months ago. I used to be a shadow of what my father wanted for me. Now, I am just myself, and I am happy.

I lie back on my bed and stare at the ceiling. Seven months ago, I tried to kill myself for the first time. Six months ago, I tried again and was nearly successful. I turn to look at my dresser, where I've started displaying pictures of my friends and trinkets from memorable times with them. I am overwhelmed by a feeling of gratitude. I'm grateful for my friends. I am grateful for my home. I am grateful for this chance to build my life into one I *want* to live.

The last few months haven't been easy. Regardless of how far I left my old life behind, I still found myself inching toward that familiar pit of despair. Sometimes I would fall in and spend days hardly leaving my room.

Following Dr. Sanchez's recommendation, I saw a psychiatrist and began taking medication for anxiety and depression. After some trial and error, I found the best dose for me. It changed everything. I continued therapy as well, and I began finding my way to the edge of the pit less often. The few times I managed to fall in, my stays inside were not as long or as overpowering as they once were.

Lung rehabilitation was brutal. I didn't realize my recovery would consist of the therapists making me wheeze on purpose. I thought it would just be breathing exercises, but they had me on a treadmill, forcing my lungs to work harder and strengthen. After I completed rehab, my doctor encouraged me to continue jogging. Rex was thrilled to have someone to run with.

Thanks to Rex's graphic design skills and my vague knowledge of social media, Marty secured enough contracts by the end of July to move me to full-time work. Now, six months later, I am helping Marty make plans to expand his business this coming spring.

Grace invites me over for dinner at least twice a month. Each time, she teaches me how to make a new dish. After dinner, we always gather around their coffee table to play games with her husband and daughters. They have practically become my new family.

Game nights with Hayden and Sierra have somehow become a Saturday night tradition. Peter and Drew join in occasionally as well. We take turns cooking or ordering food. When it is either of our turns to provide dinner, Sierra arrives early to cook with me.

I look forward to those evenings in our small kitchen, when we have to squeeze by each other, working up a glistening layer of sweat while working over the hot stove together.

We have spent months volleying flirtations. A few weeks ago, I taught her how to make muffins, and I somehow got a bit of batter on my cheek. She licked it off. My heart exploded right there in the middle of the kitchen, but neither of us has made a move since. Maybe it was my fault? I wasn't daring enough. I should have kissed her right then and there. I'm sure I fucked it up.

"Hey, Nate?" I hear from the other side of my bedroom door. "Are you almost done getting ready? We need to start cooking."

Well, speak of the devil. I stand from my bed and begin moving to the door.

"I brought you a cookie!" She says, as if I need something to lure me from my room.

I open the door to see Sierra smiling while holding up a gingerbread cookie she made to look just like me. I can't help but smile back.

"Please tell me Drew hasn't seen that."

* * *

Sierra and I are putting the finishing touches on the meal when a knock sounds at the door. Everyone we invited was already here. It is unusual to have an unannounced visitor on Christmas Eve night.

Rex yells, "Don't worry, I've got it," and opens the door only about six inches.

"Um, hi, can I help you?"

"Is Nate home?" I hear a familiar, feminine voice say.

I jolt for the door and open it wide. Standing there, looking sullen and fragile, is my mother.

"Mom?" I say, searching her face for something I wasn't sure of. "How did you find me?"

I've been ignoring her messages and calls since the day I took a medley of her pills. I wasn't entirely sure why. Maybe it was because I had finally found my way out of that dark pit, and I was worried that talking with her would drag me back to the bottom. Maybe it was because I couldn't bear her guilt on my shoulders anymore.

"I knew you and Grace had become close, and I finally got your address out of her. It took a lot of convincing, but she finally caved."

"Well, it is nice to see you." It was a lie that I desperately wanted to be true. "Merry Christmas!"

She looked at me, seeming shorter than she had before she left for her European excursion. "Merry Christmas," she says with a sad smile.

232

"Would you like to come in?" I gesture to the living room, where Hayden, Rex, Drew, Peter, and Sierra have already started piling their plates with the meal that Sierra and I had been working on most of the day. "I have friends over, but I am sure they would be happy to have you join us."

She looks over my shoulder and smiles at my friends, who are now waving at her. "No, that's alright, honey." She clears her throat and looks down at the floor. "I am going away for a while, and I had to see you before I left."

I resist the urge to say, "*What else is new?*" and let her continue.

She looks back up at me, her eyes glistening with tears. "I am leaving your father." She pauses, clearly expecting a response.

My eyebrows flick up in surprise, but that is the most I can offer. I don't know what to say.

She continues, "I'm spending some time at my sister's house and getting some help. Thank you for giving me a sign of who your father has become. I'm sorry I didn't do more to protect you from him. Or from me." She looks at her hands, now wringing in front of her. It makes me wonder if she is as naturally anxious as I am.

"He is an asshole; he didn't deserve you at all, and I'm glad you are getting the help you need." I place my hands on her shoulders and look her in the eyes. "I'm proud of you, Mom."

Her tears finally begin to fall when she throws her arms around me. "I will see you again soon, son." She kisses me on the cheek, "and when I do, I will be worthy of being your mom. I *promise*."

I kiss her on the cheek as she pulls away.

She begins to walk back down the hall, but turns, "Merry Christmas, Nate. I love you."

233

"I love you too."

I close the door behind her and lean on the frame. I close my eyes, feeling a weight I didn't realize I'd been carrying float away.

I'm not sure if it is because I'm pleased my mother is getting the help she needs or if it is because my father has lost something vital to him. Whatever it is, it makes me feel victorious.

I open my eyes and glance around my home. I take in my laughing, joyous friends, and I am overtaken by the desire to live for them—to live for *me*. Six months ago, I wanted to die. I had nothing to live for but computer games and a single, faceless friend. She pulled me along through the hardest of times. She made me see that the hard times are temporary, but the hard times *make* us. I look at Rex, who smiles at me and waves me over to the table.

I smile back and pile my plate with food.

I know I could not be here without the help of my friends. I expect the thought to make me feel worthless and weak. But I only feel human. If our roles were reversed, I'd be pissed if any of my friends tried to go through a hard time without asking for support.

I sit down on the living room couch next to Sierra and look around the small room, which is filled with people I care for as if they are my own family.

My life isn't what I expected it to be. I'm not rich, I didn't marry my high-school sweetheart, and I don't have some impressive white-collar job. But I am happy. I am me. I am loved, and learning to love myself.

* * *

Everyone clears out of the apartment by 11 p.m. Hayden had already lain down in Rex's room an hour ago after eating way too many cookies, Drew and Peter left not long after Hayden, and Sierra is preparing to drive back home. She has to be up early to go to her parents' house, but she insisted on helping me clean up before leaving.

"I'm very close to my family," she tells me as I walk with her to her car, something I have taken to doing every time she comes over. "Especially my three younger siblings. I promised them that as long as I am still living nearby, I will never miss a Christmas morning with them."

"You're lucky. I've always wanted a family like that," I admit openly.

I have been finding it easier to open up to my friends. I learned that if people care about you, they don't belittle your feelings. I have nothing to hide from them.

We arrive at her car, and she turns to look at me. Her eyes and smile shine brilliantly in the twinkling lights that the building manager strung up for the holiday season.

She puts her arms around my neck and says, "Merry Christmas, Nate." She presses against me in a hug, making something in my chest flutter. As she goes to pull away, I tighten my arms around her waist. She stays with me, staring into my eyes as I weave my fingers into her hair above her neck. I feel my heart pounding in my chest. My upper lip begins to sweat. Before I can psych myself out, I take a slow breath in, then out. Be brave, Nate.

"Merry Christmas, Sierra," I whisper just before my lips meet hers. When we part, her face is red. I can't tell if it is a blush or if she is rosy from the cold air on her skin. I can't read the look on her face. What did I do? Why the hell did I kiss her? I just ruined everything. I'll have to move. Rex would most definitely choose her over me. But what about Hayden? He would pick Rex over me, I know it. I'll lose everyone because I made one stupid move.

But then, she smiles. And kisses me back.

I let out a sigh, "Sierra, you can't do that. I thought I just royally fucked up."

She laughs, her warm breath foggy between us. "I'm sorry. I was in shock! I've wanted to kiss you for *months*."

Noticing how red her nose and cheeks are getting from standing out in the cold, I reach for her car door and open it for her. "As much as I'd like to stand here in the snow and kiss you all night. You should go home and warm up. I'll call you tomorrow."

I shut the door and turn to walk back to the sidewalk, but before she pulls out of her parking spot, I hear her window roll down. "Hey, Nate?"

I turn around and see her leaning out the window with her lips pursed, silently requesting another kiss. My god, she is so damn cute.

I jog back over to her and kiss her again. "Now get out of here, you dork."

She smiles at me, rolls up the window, and pulls away.

I shove my hands into my jacket pocket and stare off in the direction she drove. The city lights, not all that far away, feel like a beacon. I've always loved this city, but now it feels like there is something out there waiting for me. Something good.

* * *

When I return to the apartment, I find Rex sitting alone at

our small dining table with two cups of tea. She has her hands wrapped around the mug, staring into the kitchen with a faraway look in her eyes. I've done the same thing often enough that I know she is staring at nothing in particular. She is lost in her own mind.

"Can we talk?" She says with a cautious look, which I have rarely seen on her face.

"Sure." I hang my coat on the rack and ask, "What's up?"

"Would you mind sitting down?" She says, gesturing to my usual place at the table. "I made you some tea."

"Thanks." I take the seat across from her. I hold onto the mug, savoring the warmth on my frozen fingers. She stares into her cup of tea and takes three long, steadying breaths. Fuck. Did she see Sierra and me? Does she hate the idea of her two best friends together? "So, what is it?"

Before speaking, she looks me directly in the eyes. "I know your father."

I stay silent for a moment, feeling a bit confused. "Yeah, you met him at the hospital when he came to be the world's biggest dick."

I suddenly recall the way his eyes darted to the place I hadn't yet realized Rex had been sitting. I remembered the way she looked when I first saw her there. I thought it was because of me, but—

"I met him about three years ago. It was during that visit to the hospital that I knew for sure he was your father."

"What are you talking about, Quinn? Why didn't you tell me sooner?" I say, my breath becoming sharp, my lungs aching to cough.

"Because I wasn't ready before."

She pulls her phone from her pocket and slides it across the

237

table to me. When I look at the screen, I see a familiar image, a picture of a lined sheet of paper with names and numbers scrawled in black ink.

Melanie 24265

Rachel 13923

Nadya 26043

Brit 21330

Rochelle 25704

I place her phone back on the table. "Why are you showing me this?" I sit back, despair and panic taking root in my chest.

Hands shaking, she reaches forward, pointing to a name on the list. "Because *I* was Nadya, and your father is a much worse person than you know."

I swallow hard, completely lost for words.

Rex sips her tea and takes yet another deep breath. "Nate, I think it is time for me to tell you my story."

About the Author

Christina R. Adams is a proud mom, wife, and self-proclaimed goofball. With a bachelor's degree in psychology, Christina worked as a psychometrist and in human resources before embracing the adventure of being a full-time stay-at-home mom. When she's not wrangling her twin boys, Christina can be found outdoors, crafting something new, savoring a good book, or indulging in a gaming session. She enjoys antique shopping, tea-drinking, and, occasionally, squirrel-watching. Whether singing in the kitchen or exploring new hobbies, Christina brings a playful spirit and a genuine curiosity to everything she does.